Sabine Richling

The Girl and the Star

AF206108

Sabine Richling

The Girl
and
the Star

Romance Novel

Bibliografische Information der Deutschen Nationalbibliothek:
Die Deutsche Nationalbibliothek verzeichnet diese Publikation in der Deutschen Nationalbibliografie; detaillierte bibliografische Daten sind im Internet über http://dnb.dnb.de abrufbar.

Herstellung und Verlag: BoD – Books on Demand, Norderstedt

ISBN: 978-3-7504-1306-1

Persuasion doesn't work

"I really don't want to go there," I respond to Lucy. "I don't know this singer and, now that I think about it, I have something else planned."

At least, if you look at it hypothetically.

I don't think my excuse is very convincing but you can always try.

"Yes, you are going!"

Lucy puts the invitation in front of me on the table. Again, I am being persuaded, as so often. It happens to me all the time. So my fate seems sealed.

Lucy had taken part in a competition, for which this singer was the main prize. More exactly, the prize is a meal with him. She actually did win, but doesn't have the time to keep the appointment. Her boss is sending her to Germany. There she is to give a talk on the methods of archaeology at the Archaeological Institute in Hamburg. Lucy is an archaeologist. She has done a good bit of excavation. It's a really interesting profession. It's a bit related to mine. I am an ethnologist.

Viewed genetically, I am half Inuit. Other people say Eskimo. My father is an Inuit but, as far as appearance is concerned, I am the image of my Swedish mother. Her azure eyes and almost silver hair have completely dominated with me. I turned out to be a cross-breed, who does not look "blended" at all. Only the dark chocolate coloring of my father somehow transformed my skin tone into a whole milk complexion. So I am a whole milk Swede. Yet I inherited the temperament of my father. I am about as entertaining as a sleeping pill. You could say calm and introverted. Most of all, I like to sit on a block of ice and stare into the Arctic Ocean.

Since I've been living in New York, I occasionally look out the window. My computer is my best friend. I write a lot. And I'll be publishing another book in September. It will be the fifth one. My work as an ethnologist suggests what I write about. Four times, I have joined an Indian tribe for a while, observing their culture and lifestyle, actually living together with the people of a tribe. For a shy person like me, this was a challenge and a conquest.

The original inhabitants of Australia fascinate me. Unfortunately, like the Indians of North America, they live on reservations. I joined a small tribe of the Aranda and lived with them for five months in the Australian desert. It was an exciting time. Unforgettable. I wrote down my experiences in my last book. It will be on the market in two months. With my books, I want to make the public aware of abuses. I want to inform and gain the understanding of all peoples for other peoples. That is my goal.

Why am I expressing myself like this? Perhaps because I grew up in a world which was different, in which the color of my skin became a problem.

"Listen, Malina," Lucy asserts. "Isn't it clear to you who this Danny is?"

Actually not.

Innocently, I look Lucy in the eye.

"He could be the reincarnation of John Lennon and you wouldn't know it, right?"

Could be.

"Whatever. Somebody has to go. And, since I have something else to do on that day, you are the one left. He is really a dreamboat, Malina."

She holds the picture of Mr. Greyeyes to her breast and dances dreamily around the room.

I wish that I could share her joy. But you can't exactly say that I am loaded with enthusiasm. I would compare Lucy to a raging river, while I am more like a quiet, stark lake. I tend to keep my enthusiasm within limits. Especially when it concerns rock stars that I don't know and with whom I have to go eat against my expressed will.

The small village where I grew up in Greenland was so remote that half of the western world was foreign to me. After I left Greenland, something continued that had started in my childhood. It was the feeling of being strange or exotic. Since I was born, the problem has been that I am a crossbreed. I never looked like one, but rather like somebody from another planet. Fate granted my older brother Namid more luck. Our father had given it all for his bequeathing and produced an almost complete image of himself.

So much for my problem. And why was that a problem?

Children can be so cruel. Namid took his role as an older brother very seriously and regularly beat up our schoolmates to protect me from their teasing. My European appearance just didn't fit this area. Somehow I didn't fit in. At least it felt that way.

Fortunately, I didn't have to go to school forever, at least not to this one.

When my brother and I were old enough, my father showed us some important survival tricks, tied our dogs in front of the sleighs and traversed the Arctic icy wilderness with us. We learned how to build igloos and to hunt seals.

The excursions into the eternal snow and the icy world of glaciers with my father remain indelible in my memory. The loneliness, the wind, the sun; even today, I sense the solidarity with the untamed nature of the north.

Early in the game, I learned to find my way alone in the raw landscape. At the same time, the weaknesses in my character had all the time in the world to multiply. The loneliness gave me a feeling of isolation and belonged to me like a part of my body.

After seven years, the only girl friend I had acquired snatched up my only friend. Today they are married to each other.

Shortly after the disgrace of having lost my first and only friend to date to my best girlfriend, I left my native country. I wanted to study and I wanted to see the big, wide world. So I went to New York.

While in school, I met Lucy, who is my best friend today. Although I had developed a sort of "best friend trauma", I dared to take the "friend risk" again. Up until now, everything has gone well with Lucy. But then I didn't have any new boyfriend either. For the last five years, I have been without any male companionship worth mentioning.

But then there is still Lucy. We live together. Or, should I say, we share an apartment. She is always on the go. She visits conventions or goes on excavations.

Why is she forcing me to go on this date with a rock star or whatever kind of star, when the guy is absolutely unknown to me? My taste in music lags behind the spirit of the times. Do I even have one? If I am honest, I hardly know what is "in" as far as music is concerned. I don't listen to music. What is music? If Lucy is at home, I listen to her racket against my will. It might be that this singer did one of the songs she played. What was his name? Was it Danny Greyeyes? I'm supposed to meet with Danny Greyeyes. I'd prefer Brown Eyes.

"Malina, you simply have to tell me everything, you hear? You'd better bring a camera and take notes, so you don't forget anything!"

"I'm supposed to take his picture? That is really too silly."

"Naturally you'll take some pictures. Every fan would do that."

Am I a fan?

"Besides, you should definitely listen to a few of his songs so that you know what he is about."

Lucy runs to her CD rack and pulls three discs from the shelf. She comes and shoves them in my stomach.

"Here, listen and learn the titles by heart! Is that clear?"

Clear.

"Do I really have to go? I mean, don't you know anyone else who would enjoy this? Why only me?"

Lucy laughs her refreshing laugh and strokes my hair.

"Of course. But you are just the right one."

Me. How so?

"Besides, you hang out much too much with any old bush men instead of learning about real life."

So real life takes place on the stage of a rock star?

Voluntary Force

Lucy is in Hamburg. She worked on me for another day and half a night, before she left the apartment with her suitcase. But, ultimately, that wouldn't have been necessary. I would not have dared to defy her will. If Lucy decides that I should meet Mr. Greyeyes, then I will do it. Whether I want to or not.

I'm sitting on the sofa and listening to Danny's music. I like it. A little rock-like and yet gentle. My index finger is stirring around in my hair and looking for a suitable strand to wrap around it. The finger is too short. The hair rolls around the finger, twice and three times, until there is nothing more to see. I must need to shorten the hair again. Or how about longer fingers …?

The telephone startles me out of my lethargy.

"Hello, are you Miss Lucy Atkinson?" A hollow voice echoes from the receiver directly into my ear canal.

"No, she is not here. My name is Malina Bergstroem. Maybe I can help you?"

Quiet. Crackle. Rustle. Whispering.

"Do you know when she can be reached?"

"Not for three days," I reply. "What is this about and with whom am I speaking?" Quiet. Crackle. Rustle. Whispering.

"My name is Adam Fox. I am Danny Greyeyes' manager. To our knowledge, Miss Atkinson won the main prize. A dinner with Danny.

Do you know anything about that? I wanted to arrange the formalities with her."

"Well. You will have to arrange those with me. Miss Atkinson transferred her prize to me."

Quiet. Crackle. Rustle. Whispering.

"Good. Then will you reveal your name?"

"My name is Malina Bergstroem."

I feel my pulse everywhere. I really don't want to do that. But could I disappoint Lucy? Could I willfully disappoint any person at all? Besides myself. I disappoint myself continuously. Because I never manage to assert my own will. I'd rather give in to another person's will. It's easier.

Mr. Adam Fox explains the course of the meeting with Danny Greyeyes to me. When I have to say what and how I have to look into the camera. Which answers I must give the Star Magazine and the clothing I should best wear.

"Be punctual, Miss Bergstroem. Tomorrow at 5 o'clock in the studios of the Megastar record company."

Is it really tomorrow? Can't we postpone the whole thing until next week? Or next year?

"Yes," I hear myself mutter into the receiver.

Great!

I start the next day with restless running around the apartment. I can't even think about breakfast. Where would I put it? My stomach is gone. It has slipped to my knees. And my closet is not coughing up any suitable clothes. Since when am I a normal woman? I plod into Lucy's room and rifle through her wardrobe. A dress. Black. Short. Spaghetti straps. Decent but stylish. I'll take it.

The telephone rings. Lucy!

"Hi, Malina. Don't even think about missing the appointment. And don't forget the camera! I envy you so much."

I'm fine, thanks, and you?

"Then come on and go yourself! I'll fill in for you in Hamburg."

"Oh, Malina, if that would only work. But if there is anybody I don't begrudge getting this chance, it is you."

Oh, how touching. Why don't I feel like I am indulging myself?

I explain to Lucy about the conversation with Mr. Adam Fox and the planned order of events. Photo-shootings, interviews, posing for the camera with Danny Greyeyes, and finally the long-desired dinner in cozy togetherness, without cameras and witnesses. What will I talk about with him? I hope my mouth will open up and say something. I ask Lucy what sort of conversation would work for a rock star. Lucy laughs.

"Why don't you take it as it comes? Some kind of conversation will result."

Good tip. Why didn't I think of it myself?

After the phone conversation with Lucy, I don't feel any better. The hands of the clock seem to be competing against each other. Time is racing at a breakneck speed. It's always when you don't need it. At the last minute I rush into the bathroom and throw myself under the shower. Fresh but unfortunately not a new person, I get out and occupy myself with Lucy's dress. It seems to fit. I blow dry my stubborn hair as I keep looking at the clock. Damn, I have to get going. I don't want to go. I don't want to!

The hair I just dried flies through the air in an arc over my head, landing in light waves on my back. Shoes. Where are the shoes? Grab for the purse. Don't need a jacket. Warm outside. Whizz down the stairs. Find the car. Drive off with squeaking tires. Pulse at 180.

Without even noticing, I arrive. At Megastar. My thoughts are all jumbled up and I cannot concentrate on the here and now. So I don't notice that I am driving by the place. By Megastar. Darn, where am I? Oops. The light was red. What am I saying? How am I reacting? What if they get wise that I have no idea about Danny and his Greyeyes? Wait a minute, wasn't that the building? Of Megastar? U-turn. Please let me in! I'm in a hurry. Somebody honks. The driver of the honking vehicle waves at me. I wave back. Looked like a long finger. Jerk!

A parking place. Right in front of the building. Thank God!

I get out of my car and just notice an uncontrollable crowd of people in front of the entrance.

Where are they headed? Apparently there's no getting through this gathering. I linger briefly with the crowd and consider a plan for getting into the building quickly. The door is blocked by two athletic guards. Then I have the idea of brutally attacking the entrance, clearing out the people with a punch, and knocking down the guards. Maybe something better will occur to me. Maybe there is a back entrance. But where? Doubtfully, I look around. An entrance. To a courtyard behind the building. The conditions are good for a back entrance. Unnoticed, I break away from the mutiny and, invisible, stroll the "back way to the back courtyard" so as to reach the expected back entrance. There! I was right. Just found the courtyard door. If there is no blood hound with baring teeth and huge jaws awaiting me, I could succeed in continuing my way into the building to Mr. Greyeyes. When I open it, the door squeaks like a piece of chalk being pulled over the surface of a blackboard. I have to shake myself.

I step through the door, which is like a portal to a cave, and find myself in a pitch dark stairwell. No dog in the vicinity.

The way to my destination is paved by metal steps. I can't see them, but the lingering echo of my steps gives it away.

I hear somebody tramping down from above. The steps are gaining in speed. And suddenly I see it. The shapeless figure comes at me like a freight train. Helpless, I sense that it is not possible to get out of the way. The figure doesn't notice me and does not reduce its speed. Motionless like a statue, I hold on to the railing in the hope of thwarting a fall. Through squinting eyes, I sense the shock of the inevitable collision. A severe pain in my head suggests what has just happened. At the same time, my hand is torn from the railing. The figure and I fall a few metal steps downward.

"For God's sakes!" the figure, lying on me with all his weight, calls out. I feel like I've been ironed against my will. Like a dried fig leaf between the pages of a thick book. My left foot is caught in a trouser leg. It can't be my own. I have a dress on. My right arm seems twisted like a cord and is touching a strange arm, which is lingering below my back and touching my backside. If there was a way to untie this knot, I would like to have known it.

My lips cannot utter even a word. The warm breath of the figure wanders through my cleavage and releases the aroma of pizza and garlic. Long hair is tickling my face. And it is not mine. Now the figure pulls out its warm arm from behind my back and speaks to me.

"Is everything okay with you?"

"I think so."

Aha, the form seems to be of male origin. The voice gave it away.

"Damn, that is just typical for this day!" he says in a disgruntled way.

Concerned, I try to concentrate on my arms as the male figure slowly moves away from me. I find the one arm but not the other one. In the dim light, I discern a right hand being extended to me and I consider grabbing it. Where is my right arm? Alternatively, I hold my left arm toward the hand, which grabs it right off and lifts me on my feet. Shortly thereafter I find the right arm. Slowly the feeling comes back. I sense a tingling.

"Sorry but I simply didn't see you. But it's damned dark in this place. Isn't there any damned light here?"

"Damned" seems to be his favorite word.

"Sorry, but I desperately need to get going. Have a silly meeting with a broad I don't know. Is everything really all right with you?"

"Yes, thank you."

The male figure nods and continues his way downstairs, then suddenly pauses and turns to me. As if somebody had pulled the plug from the power supply, he stands there motionless and looks at me. Why he is looking so mysteriously? In this "damned" darkness, he can't tell anything about me anyway. My fingers are fidgeting nervously. Should I say something else? No, now he is going on.

After the intense mishap, I climb the stairs, hesitating and at a snail's pace so as to avoid another fall. In the case of another incident, I am gaining time to figure how to get out of the way. Finally I reach a bright hallway. From afar, I hear a lot of hubbub with different sounds. It is like a tree full of little bickering sparrows. The sound of steps being taken comes toward me. Suspicious of what could be awaiting me, I keep myself close to the wall. A woman, elegantly dressed, enters my field of vision and prances toward me in her high heeled shoes.

"Oh, there you are, finally!" she calls out.

I turn around, look at her again and point to myself with my index finger.

"But you are the girl who gets to meet her great heartthrob today? Miss Bergstroem?"

The girl! Does she think I'm a teenager?

"Yes, that is me."

"Then come quickly! Shoo! We still have to have you styled for the photo-shoot with Danny."

My goodness! What are they doing with me?

She grabs my strained arm and drags me down the hall. We remain standing at room number 21. Energetically, she pushes on the door, which is ajar, and a team of stylists and hairdressers storms toward me. They are all babbling wildly and pulling on me. Each knows exactly what sort of manual dexterity he must use on me. They pull me onto a chair and, before I can even make a sound, the soft bristles of a large brush dust off my face and tickle my nose. One hand applies mascara to my eyelids and another backcombs my hair. The next one paints my fingernails. A little here, a little there. Just don't look in the mirror. Who knows what will come of it?

Can't they just leave me like I am? What can they object to about my appearance? It's completely okay. The high heel lady rushes back into the room.

"Hurry, people! Time is short. Aren't you finished with her yet?"

Exactly, what are you doing with me for so long? They act as if I needed a complete makeover. Now they're applying lipstick. Yuck!

I'm asked to look in the mirror. The overhaul seems to be complete. Why do they look so delighted, as if I were the mother of a new born baby? For God's sake, what have they done to me? Astounded, I look in the mirror with my mouth wide open. Good, I have to admit, it's not bad at all. But … where am I? I mean ME!

The high heels come at me again. She lifts her hands to her face.

"Wow, girl! You are a real beauty."

They all look at me as if I were the all-time masterpiece of their work.

"Come on! Let's get going."

High heel lady grabs me by the arm and pulls me out of the chair. Be careful, that is the injured arm. I could say it out loud. But that won't work. My mouth is sticky with lipstick.

We go along the hall to room 13. The door opens and − people again. Too many for my taste. I wish I were on a lonely ice floe. But that isn't possible. I'm still in room 13.

"I haven't even introduced myself. You can call me Helen. I'll be coaching you today. What was your name?"

"Malina," I answer quietly.

"Oh, right. So, people. Listen up. This is Malina. First you'll take a few pictures of her. And – where is Danny?"

"Here I am!"

The sentence came without any warning.

Helen and I turn around and see what I must admit is a scrumptious man coming through the door; with him is the pizza-garlic breath. There is a question mark in my mind. The figure from the stairwell? Danny Greyeyes, the pizza figure?

"Hey, Malina, how's it going?"

He comes directly to me and reaches out his arms. I turn around anxiously and check whether I should get out of the way for someone else. But there is nobody. Only me. For the cameras, he briefly takes me in his arms. There is flashing and clicking from all sides. He smiles a few times into the camera before, cool as can be, he turns away from me.

He didn't recognize me. It would have been the same for me, had he not just inhaled a pizza with an extra measure of garlic.

I look at him more carefully. His dark, shoulder-length hair is restrained by the sunglasses he is wearing. His jeans emphasize his sexy backside, while the blue shirt hangs casually over his pants. His eyes seem as dark as the stairwell, in which we got knotted together. He is definitely of Indian ancestry. Is that the reason why Lucy appointed me for this meeting?

He whispers something to "High Heels Helen". Doubtlessly nothing pleasant. You might think he was somewhat irritated. Be quieter there in the background. I would like to understand some of this. Intensely, I try to read lips. That could have been "not in the mood". It's the same for me. So then I can go now. Excuse me, where is the exit here? I'm not in the mood either. Carefully, I sneak to the door and turn inconspicuously to all sides. Nobody notices me. They are all looking at Mr. Greyeyes. Soon I will have reached the door and then I am free again.

"Stop! Where do you want to go?"

Helen has discovered me and immediately detached herself from Danny. How many eyes does this woman have?

"Please take care of Malina! You can take the first pictures of her."

Danny looks over to me and examines me from top to bottom. I try to avoid his gaze and think of an ice floe. But even the little man, who is moving toward me with a swing of the hips, cannot separate me from this gaze. Can't Mr. Greyeyes look somewhere else? Just don't pay any attention to him. Think of a bluish white iceberg, which is peacefully rolling by you. The little man places me on a cold chair in front of a screen. Danny is not looking any more. Pooh!

"Oh, your mascara is crumbling," the man says indignantly with a feminine tone of voice. He wiggles off, waving his hands, only to return with a soft cloth.

"So, Malinachen, stretch out your little nose!"

Bravely, I do what he says. This place is swarming with crazy people. I must see that I can get out of here in good shape.

I get instructions on how I need to place myself on the chair from all sides. The head up and then the head down again. The back straight. Put hair to the side and then to the other side. Click. Flash. Flash. Klick. Flash. Put your arms on your hips. Now the hair to the back. Flash. Click. Flash. Flash. And smile again. Flash. Flash.

I think of my parents. It's time that I call them. I miss them. My brother is also living in New York but we have no regular contact. He strays from one part of the city to the next and has been studying something new for years.

I don't want to commit myself, he had once answered, when I anxiously addressed the subject.

"Malinalein, please look into the camera!" the little man reprimands me.

My attention wanders to Danny Greyeyes. He is staying at the other end of the room, surrounded by some people. What kind of strange second encounter was that with him? He doesn't think much of his fans. Well, I am no fan, but you don't see that at a glance. Or do you?

"Here is the little bird. Hey, come here, cooee!"

I don't know into which lens I should first look. It's flashing from all sides.

"Little mouse, if you are posing for a camera, you must also look into it."

One?

"Being a photo model means thinking, feeling and being on the ball, dear."

Blankly, the little man shakes his head.

"But I'm not a photo model," I protest.

"Oh, little one. Certainly you are one, at least from now on. Do you seriously believe I would let a face like yours go away? By the way, I am Charles. My friends call me Charley."

The little man extends his delicate hand.

Model – me? What an abstruse idea! Where is my ice floe?

"So, people …", "High Heels Helen" claps her hands to get it quiet, "now we will take a few pictures with the two of them together. Danny, please come on."

Danny Greyeyes looks through the circle of people surrounding him and curls one eyebrow.

"OK, boss, be right there."

He proceeds over to me and places himself directly next to me. Together we blink into the cameras. Once into the one and then into the other. Danny's hand grasps my shoulder. Flash. Flash. Click.

"Look each other in the eyes!" Charley directs us.

Honestly, I would rather go now. Thank you, it was nice. Look in his eyes. How is that supposed to work? I am already agitated enough and just manage to hold my head in an upright position. Otherwise, I am as stiff as the parquet floor in this room. Ever tried to move a stiff neck? Simply nothing happens. However much you try. Mr. Greyeyes is looking at me. I can sense it. But my head doesn't move.

"But, Malinchen, don't make such a fuss! Look your heartthrob in the eye!"

Heartthrob? Could my heartthrob take his hand from my shoulder? Maybe then I could succeed in swinging around with my upper body. Hand still resting on shoulder.

"Malina, dear, what is it?"

All at once, Danny Greyeyes' hands grab me by the shoulder and turn me around to him.

Thanks. I couldn't have done that on my own, Numb, I look from one Browneye into the other. Back and forth. I can't decide on either one. This expression. It's running hot and cold down my back. His mouth changes to a deep smile. I can't smile. I'm still completely thunderstruck. A glass of water would be useful. I feel so different. I sense how my empty stomach is contracting in pain. It won't digest itself? It wasn't a good idea not to have breakfast and leave out lunch.

"Smile, you two." Charley is relentless.

Click. Flash. Click. Flash.

"Danny, put your arms around Malina's hips and keep looking into her eyes, all right?"

No, I can't take this. I don't like to be embraced by strange men. Even if their name is Greyeyes. I feel sick.

How about something edible? Oh, what wonderful shapes are appearing before my eyes! A white haze adorns my field of vision with the most diverse patterns and is gradually transformed into darkness.

After a while, I perceive excited voices. Where am I? Where is the dissonant chanting coming from? Am I at home? Thousands of tiny fire ants are crawling on my legs and arms. I open my eyes. Slowly an image is formed. I sense what has just happened. My sight gets clearer. Soon I recognize the face with the Browneyes above me.

"She's coming to again."

"Oh, thank God!" Charley is scrambling. "Child, what are you doing? A glass of water! Fast!"

Charley lifts up my head and puts a glass of water to my mouth. The cool liquid runs down my esophagus and revives my senses.

"Probably everything was a bit too much for you right at the beginning."

Sympathetically, Charley strokes my hair.

Yes, you could say that. But it could be my empty stomach causing my condition to deteriorate.

I then get to spend some time resting on a couch. Helen has decided to stop the photo shoot immediately and, after a short break, move on to the interview. There is a dry piece of bread on the table in front of me. It's for me. With my stomach rumbling, I had asked for a little energy booster and they turned the whole studio upside down, searching for some nourishment. One of the lighting technicians found some bread in his pocket. It now belongs to me. I'm not hungry but reason tells me to put something in my stomach. Danny has gotten lost. At least I can't locate him among all these people. That's good also. I have as little interest in him as he does in me. What did he say to me before in the stairwell? He had a silly meeting with a broad. I am that broad.

The (Un-) Desired Dinner

Meanwhile, I am in room number 9. The interview with the lady from Star Magazine seems to be nearing the end, and I haven't answered the question of what I am here for. Until now, no one has spoken to me one single time. The interview is just with Mr. Greyeyes. Of course! Why should they want to interview me? In their eyes, I am an unknown quantity. "Miss Bergstroem …" Startled, I sit up and, after the lapse in my thoughts, I am again tuned in. Mrs. "Star Magazine" actually does speak to me.

"How long have you fancied Danny Greyeyes?"

I? Fancy? What is she talking about? Do I have to answer?

Helen, who is sitting next to me, pokes me in the side. But that doesn't help me. Nothing clever occurs to me.

"For some time," I hear myself answer.

Mild laughter of those present penetrates the room.

"And which songs do you like the most, Miss Bergstrom?"

Luuuuucyyyy! What have you gotten me into? What were the names of those dumb songs? I had learned them by heart. In any case, I knew some of them. Honest. But now … they no longer come to mind. They have disappeared from my brain.

Danny Greyeyes looks over at me attentively.

"All of them," I answer mechanically.

"Oh yes. You are really a dyed-in-the-wool fan, aren't you?"

"Oh, certainly."

Fan. Dyed-in-the-wool. Me. Maybe I should write a book about this experience, with the title "My Friend Lucy Throws Me to the Wolves".

"So, that's fine. I am about finished with my interview. Do you still have questions for Danny, Miss Bergstroem?"

Mrs. "Star Magazine" winks at me as if she wanted to say: "Now, girl, this is your chance. Ask him everything you always wanted to know about him!" Nonetheless, I have no questions. Only want to get away. I shake my head.

Somewhat later, I am sitting in room 3. Helen is planning with Adam Fox, who just arrived, for the intimate dinner with me and Danny's "brown eyes". Charley is sitting next to me and trying to talk me into a contract for photo modeling.

"Dear, I am offering you the chance of a lifetime. Your face simply must go on all the magazine covers and you know that."

I know nothing of the kind.

Suddenly Danny is standing in the doorframe. He looks over at us and shakes his head.

What is that supposed to mean? What gives him the right to simply shake his head? I don't find it so great to have to go eat with him. At most, my stomach, but I certainly don't. So he doesn't need to look over at me so disparagingly and shake his head. Finally he marches off, and I feel somewhat freer.

"You just need to sign down here, and then we can get underway next week. What do you say, little one?"

"I'm sorry. But that is nothing for me," I answer flatly.

"So you're declining? Helen, did you get that? The girl is refusing to be photographed by me."

Helen looks over to me.

"You aren't serious, child. Do you know how many young girls dream of this? You only get one chance at something like this in life. With the money you earn, you would suddenly have limitless possibilities."

"I am not short of money, and my dreams involve other things. Nonetheless, thank you for the offer."

Mr. Adam Fox laughs.

"What an unusual reaction, Miss Bergstroem. I am impressed. You are probably the only woman on earth with the courage to turn down such an offer. May I ask why?"

I am impressed myself. For the first time, I did not allow something to be imposed on me. Lucy would be proud of me. How did I pull that off?

"Why did you become a manager and not an auto mechanic?"

My question in response seems to satisfy him. He smiles at me and nods his head.

If only everything were over. I simply can't deal with so much hullabaloo about my person.

On the ride to the restaurant, I sit across from Danny Greyeyes in the stretch limo, without the contract for modeling. He is conversing excitedly with the camera man and a photographer, while Helen is on the phone continuously. How I long for peaceful quiet. I imagine a snowy landscape. Gently the snow trickles on the ground and softens every sound into nothing. Unfortunately, this chaos of conversation is penetrating my virgin ear canal. The camera's constant flurry of camera flashes hampers the colored rods in my eyes from performing their work. I see black spots in my field of vision. The video camera is recording continuously.

Soon we will stop at a posh restaurant, where the intimate dinner with Danny will take place. I probably won't be able to eat a bite. How could I when, with all this agitation, I can't open my mouth to speak? My hands can speak better than I. I write down everything that I have to say. Practically speaking, my books are my voice.

My publisher recognized this immediately. When I sat across from him with my first manuscript and had absolutely nothing to say to him, since everything about me was in this first book, he just laughed and nodded his head. We have never regretted the collaboration. I write, he publishes, and the people buy. We hardly have to talk with each other. I receive the checks in the mail. I am content with this. I would be fine without words, but society is designed for pure communication. At the baker's, at the ticket counter, at the barber's – you have to say something everywhere.

Full of interest, I inspect the face of Danny Greyeyes. Pleasant wrinkles appear around his fascinating brown eyes when he laughs. On his forehead, a few dimples bury themselves into the skin between the eyebrows. He has a facial expression which gives a high principled effect. I suspect he is in his mid-thirties. I had imagined him to be younger.

Shortly after the car has reached its destination, everyone gets out of the vehicle. Inevitably, I am the one who gets out last. With a wide grin, the camera man helps me out of the seat into his camera-free arm. Was that a sexual advance? I remember his many lecherous looks in the car. I had tactfully overlooked them. With a discerning dimples look, Danny Greyeyes looks over. Quickly, I work my way out of the offensive arm.

We are in front of the restaurant, and it has an unsettling effect on me. I can literally hear the cries of the lobsters and crabs struggling for their life in the boiling water. The prices on the menu likely exceed the height of the Eifel Tower, if there even is a menu.

Helen turns to me.

"Come over here, child!"

I come.

"The owner of the restaurant knows that we are taking a few pictures of you at the table. Then we will disappear, leaving you to your fate. Ha, ha."

I feel completely stupid. It seems no different for Danny. His dimples get deeper, and his tired glance moves to the floor. He casually buries his hands in his pockets and goes through the door in front of me.

The table prepared is in a cozy corner. The camera man wildly starts taking pictures. No, Mr. Danny Greyeyes is not courteous enough to adjust my chair. Without a word, he sits down at the table and looks around. We are served two glasses of champagne and the candles are lit. Helen asks us to smile and look into the camera.

I admit that the meeting is silly, Mr. Greyeyes, but the "broad" Malina isn't really responsible. The circus being staged here wasn't my idea. Danny is really unfortunate. How can somebody willingly want to be a star?

Finally, the bustle subsides. Helen and the camera team leave the restaurant after a short farewell and an ambiguous wink of the eye. My feet are wobbling inconspicuously. How can I start a conversation with someone, for whom I was nothing but air until now? My uneasiness, which grows enormously, when I have to converse with unknown persons, causes me to fall silent. Danny Greyeyes makes a start.

"So, now we are rid of them."

I nod in agreement.

"It was an exciting day for you? Something you don't experience every day, right?"

Nod again.

Maybe I should say something?

The appetizer is served – fortunately – so maybe my silence won't stand out so much. We both reach for the bread. Our hands meet in the bread basket. Embarrassed, I immediately pull my hand away.

"But no, please!" Danny holds the bread basket under my nose. Cautiously, I take out a piece.

"Tell me. What sort of work do you do?"

He asks me? Wouldn't that be my part, as a dyed-in-the-wool fan? I hardly think that a rock star is interested in my life. Certainly not when it has taken place mostly on a far distant and lonely island like Greenland.

I would like to talk about something, but what? What do I do? Write books and work on ethnology. Well, I did give an interview one time. I was asked about my books and knew ahead exactly what I had to answer. For the answer I would need a little more preparation time. I would have to first make some notes and plan each word deliberately. I can't make an impromptu report about what I do.

"You don't like to talk so much? Doesn't matter. I don't mind if we get on with this nonsense as quickly as possible. My manager thought it wouldn't hurt my image if I could benefit from a little publicity. That's why there was all the fuss today."

Aha!

"And you seem to be profiting from it. Wow! You signed a photo modeling contract right off. Congratulations! Something could come of it. You're not bad looking at all."

Thank you.

The main course is served.

I would like to rectify something but I don't want to interrupt his flow of words.

"You set a tremendous pace. In the past, almost every one of my girlfriends had an advertising contract or a small film role in her pocket. For you, a few hours in the buildings of my record company are enough, without our even knowing each other. You women are really amazing. If you can't get something with your head, then try with Vitamin B or – well, no comment!"

The ignition button of the explosive in my stomach was triggered. To avoid an explosion, I think about leaving.

"I don't need the help of other people to make something of my life," I hear myself say, completely peeved.

Danny looks up and curls the furrows on his forehead, which deepens the dimples between his eyebrows.

"You would be the first woman I've encountered who thinks that way. My experience is quite different. I could never be certain whether a woman wanted something from me or my money and fame. That's how it is in my business. Lies and deception."

"Why don't you simply start from the beginning and begin a new life where nobody knows you?" I ask.

With a cynical smile, he looks at me blankly.

"How wonderfully naïve you are. Apparently you don't know much about life. You are just a young thing."

Insulted, I sit up and take notice. Naivety is a word that in no way describes my character. How does he get that? In my view, life experience depends on the number of experiences and is not necessarily proportional to age.

"Believe me, it doesn't matter where you go. It will catch up with you everywhere. No place is safe from the life that is determined for you," he suddenly muses. "You are likely the baby of the family. You grew up sheltered and with many friends, and much consumption."

Where does he get this information? Do I have to have a scroll pasted on my forehead?

"Wait, let me guess – you like to go to the disco, right?"

Astonished how he gains so much speculative knowledge about me, I thoughtfully scratch my head. I would like to have put my personality in the right light; but the thought of saying "no, that's not right at all" is too simple and wouldn't have corrected his false image of me.

"So I am right. It's okay. Most girls your age lead an innocent life and are only interested in their appearance."

Our plates are removed and more champagne is poured, so that Danny has to interrupt his comments. I briefly consider objecting loudly. But why should I prevent him from thinking that way about me? I would never have thought that a quiet person like me could be taken for a wild disco fan. Somehow has something to it.

When the waiter has left the table, I still try to use my chance for denials. I take a deep breath but Danny is faster.

"Why did you collapse earlier in the studio? Well, you wouldn't be the first girl to faint just because I walk by. I simply don't understand you women. It would be nice to meet one who is different from all the others."

Actually, you were not the reason but – it was my stomach …

"Maybe it has to do with you and not the women that you always encounter the same ones."

I pat myself on the back for my daring advance in this previously one-sided discussion.

"How am I to understand that?" he asks, feeling snubbed.

"Maybe you only see what you expect."

Danny Greyeyes leans forward. The sudden proximity to his face unsettles me, so I move back a bit.

Before he can respond, the desert is served. Happily I grab for it. I have to bridge this pause in the conversation, so I quickly gobble down the food.

When we are alone again, Danny shakes his head intensely.

"Talking to you is fun. Barely out of diapers and already juggling with precocious observations, whose meaning you don't understand."

The desert plops heavily into my stomach. I swallowed too fast and forgot to chew. Or is his disrespectful comment on my knowledge about questions of life pressing on my stomach?

"How old are you, girl?"

Girl! I always knew that I seem younger to other people but my time as a girl is unfortunately over.

"Twenty eight," I answer truthfully.

A smile, with the left corner of his mouth going upward, hints that he doesn't believe me. Should I have said nineteen?

"It's okay. You don't need to divulge your true age."

I find it charming to be thought of as so young, but apparently he assesses the maturity of character by age. And, if he thinks I'm nineteen, I don't possess much of it in his eyes.

"Well, how old are you?" I ask in my ill-humored way. My voice has reached an unexpected volume and almost cracks. "No, let me guess. Probably just over sixty. Apparently you can draw on a treasure of wisdom, about which others can only dream. Am I on target?"

I blink and smile affectedly. My snippy tone of voice is new to me. I wasn't aware that I could do that.

He folds his arms and looks at me through squinty eyes.

"You surprise me."

I surprise myself.

"You are really thawing out. I thought that conversation with you wasn't possible."

It really isn't.

"Actually, you should know that I am thirty eight. Most fans are better informed than I am. I understand what you wanted to tell me. Maybe I am underestimating you."

"Yes, maybe."

"Well, I am just a person, and I have my weaknesses. Maybe you are right and I judge people falsely. Not so stupid of you."

I know.

"Just see people as they are and remain unbiased. Otherwise, you will not get a clear image."

My father gave me this bit of wisdom back then. Sometimes it has helped me. A little bit.

Mr. Greyeyes hasn't even touched his desert. Perhaps I could …

The hole in my stomach was bigger than I thought. Whether I should ask him? He takes his spoon in his hand and plays with it. Is he going to eat the desert or not?

The ambiguous look he gives me highlights his dimples.

"I can't figure you out. At the moment, you are giving the impression that you bear the weight of the whole world on your shoulders. What do you want to know? I have my reasons for not being unbiased toward people. If you had lived my life, you would know what I am talking about. I lost my parents at the age of fourteen. I spent the rest of my childhood in an orphanage, in which no child was like me. Do you understand what I mean? No, you can't at all. Look at you. Blond and blue eyed like a little doll. Brown from a tanning salon. How laughable."

A tanning salon? I have never been under a sun lamp in my life.

"If I had led a life like yours, then I too could sprout such pseudo-sanctimonious pearls of wisdom," he adds to his last frosty comments.

How does he know what kind of a life I have led? I can't remember having told anything of my life. I have never met a person who is afflicted with so many biases as this Danny Greyeyes. What causes a person to think this way?

"I don't expect that you understand that," he continues his attack, undeterred. "You can't understand how it is to be different than the others. To be discriminated against, just on account of your skin color. I would like to have had it as easy as you."

I have lost my appetite for Danny's desert. I am happy that I am not as embittered as he is. Of course, I can't seriously judge how bad it was for him in his childhood; but I admit that I cannot really comprehend his bitterness. I have met people who were doing significantly worse and who didn't complain at all.

"You seem to be a rather dissatisfied person. I'm sorry. But don't you think it would be better for you to let go of the experiences from the past? That is all behind you. Why don't you concentrate on life at the moment?"

I replied a little too quickly. My thoughts just popped out of my mouth. Normally, I keep them to myself.

His unpleasant laugh reveals that I have dared too much.

"And a little calculating lady, who is out to become a photo model, and has no idea how it feels to be an outsider because of his skin color tells me this? Spare me your clever advice and mind your own business!'

His spoon bangs on the table. The glass next to it shatters into a thousand tiny slivers. Fortunately, it is empty.

Startled, I jerk back from fright.

"Thank you for the empathetic words. At this point, we should end the evening. It's nice to have met you."

I feel misunderstood. What have I said that would justify such a reaction? Shouldn't I be the one to take off in a huff? After all, he's the one who mercilessly judged me, although he knows absolutely nothing about me.

Furious, he gets up from his chair and stomps out of the restaurant, without so much as a glance. Puzzled, I look after him.

Okay, what now?

Danny's unexpected departure completely confused me. He surely expected more empathy on my part. Should I have not been so direct? It is his past and has nothing at all to do with mine. Nonetheless, I admit having encountered some parallels. Unconsciously, I projected myself and my experiences onto his. That was ill-considered.

A waiter hurries to the table and excuses himself for the shattered glass. How does he figure that? As if he was responsible for it. He asks if he should bring a new one. I thank him politely and explain that I intend to go as well.

"Bella Signorina, those are not good manners from Signor Greyeyes. You don't treat a bella lady like that. In Italy, we put our women on a pedestal."

Of course, the Italians don't place their women on a pedestal any more than other men, but the waiter's comforting words bring a smile to my face.

Depressed, I step out the door and look at a dark street empty of people. My car is still in front of the gates of the Megastar Company and I have practically no idea in what corner of New York I am right now. I would like to wave down a taxi, but not even a bicycle goes by. A cool evening breeze is blowing. The air smells damp. Surely there will be rain. I cross my arms in front of my chest to provide a little warmth. Slowly I move along and look thoughtfully at the ground. Continuously, I think of the sudden departure of Danny Greyeyes and go over the sentences of our discussion again and again. I would like to understand what I did wrong.

Suddenly, I hear fast steps behind me. It wouldn't be wise to turn around. I hold on tight to my handbag. I become conscious of the dark and this deserted area. Only now do I realize how helpless I am in this situation and how easy an assault on me would be. Even though loneliness was my best friend in Greenland, you should take care in large city like New York. Here it is advisable, especially as a woman, never to wander alone through narrow streets. In front of me, I can make out a well-lit intersection. A main street. Lots of cars. The steps behind me are getting closer. I increase my speed. In the distance, I see a few people. In a moment, I will have made it. But a hand grabs my shoulder and prevents me from fleeing.

"No!!!" I cry out, terrified, and strike around me with my hand bag, while I turn around.

A dark male figure again tries to grab for me. Accurately, I strike a few blows with my bag. As he ducks down, I hope for my chance to escape.

"Stop it!" the figure calls out to me. I'm not about to and try to give my punches a little more spin. But now the figure is reaching more powerfully toward me and pushes me against the wall of houses.

"Damn it, will you finally stop that!" a voice screams out, which sounds familiar to me. I bring the clash to a halt and, in the gloomy reflection of the street light, I recognize the face of Danny Greyeyes. Completely out of breath from our skirmish, we stand opposite each other. I try to find the reason for his reappearance in his eyes but it is too dark.

"I'm sorry if I startled you." Danny's voice suddenly breaks through the silence. It's not a question of being startled; I was in mortal fear.

"It's fine," I answer, as if everything had been only half as wild.

"Really?"

I nod.

A shiver runs down my spine. I don't know whether the proximity to Danny Greyeyes caused this or the cold air on this evening, which goes right through me. As I stand there with my teeth chattering, I am still pressed against the wall by Danny.

"Now I recognize you again," he remarks, somewhat stunned.

Yes, I am the nineteen year old girl who sat with you in this posh *but warm restaurant. Could I please go home now?*

"How nice it is that you recognize me after such a short time. That doesn't happen to me often," I say derisively.

Danny laughs and his hair goes back and forth.

"You collided with me on the stairs. That was you."

His glance deeply penetrates my eyes.

"I have to encounter you again in the dark to recognize you. What irony."

He must come from northern Greenland. There you learn as a child to find your way in the eternal darkness of winter.

"I would like to go on now; otherwise, I will be glued to the wall you are pushing me against," I say with a shiver. Hardly have I spoken the last word and I am pulled onto the sidewalk.

"Excuse me! You are right. I'll take you home or you will catch cold in your delicate little dress."

Transformed into the solicitous gentleman, he takes off his jacket and puts it over my shoulders. His body warmth seems to have gathered itself in this jacket, since it is so warm, as if it had been hanging over a heater.

"Better?" he asks solicitously.

"Yes, thank you. That's much better."

Silently, we walk next to each other for a while down the way.

"I thought you were long gone. Why are you still here?" I ask some time later.

My question seems to make him uneasy, as he runs his hands through his hair several times.

"Honestly speaking, I had only gone a few steps until the cool air provided me with a clear head. I had a bad conscience, since I had left you back in the restaurant. So I went back and waited for you behind the door. It became clear to me that you were right with what you said. I just didn't want to admit it. Your direct manner is not something I'm used to. It was puzzling why I immediately spoke with you about my past. I usually don't talk about it. At least not so fast. You are the first person who didn't show sympathy. It insulted me a little bit."

Ashamed, I look at the ground and sense how my bad conscience is gnawing at me. So I was right. Empathy is not my strong suit. I must definitely work on this character flaw. It is not my intention to offend other people after a short encounter.

"I'm sorry. I had no feeling for your sensitivity," I apologized.

Unexpectedly, Danny jumps in the way and stops me by grabbing my shoulders.

"I was the one without any tact toward you. The whole time, I failed to take you seriously, and I was arrogant and presumptuous. If someone has to apologize, then it is me. You had to take a lot. It is not easy to provoke you."

Actually it is. I'm just too reserved to protest.

My body is being transformed into jelly. My legs are trembling in tandem with my arms. It is much too cool for a summer evening.

"Hey, you are freezing. Come here!" Danny takes me in his arms. I am completely confused about his actions. His hands are warming me, rubbing over my back. A taxi turns into our street.

Just at this moment. Should I say something and distract him from providing me warmth? For the first time in a long time, I enjoy being close to another person. I didn't know that it can be so nice. Memories are awakening.

The taxi crawls along like a big, yellow turtle. When did it roll by us? Now he also sees it. Silently, he looks at it and continues rubbing my back. It was not important to him either. Now it's gone.

"Are you getting warmer?" he asks innocently, as if his rubbing was the only thing in the world that could keep me from freezing.

"Yes," I fib. Don't know why. Maybe I hope to be warmed this way more often in the future.

"You are going to burn me," he whispers, smiling. "Your lips are already blue."

How can he tell that in this darkness? I admire his good vision. We smile at each other.

"I have constantly been thinking about the encounter with you in the stairwell. If I had only known that it was you ..."

"Would you have been friendlier to me?" I ask without inhibitions.

He continues talking as if he had not heard my question.

"There was something with you on this step. You radiate something."

What then? I radiate what? Am I radioactive? His warm thumb moves over my lips. My uneasiness gives way to a new feeling, which warms me from inside. So I forget that I am cold, forget the lonely street, forget everything around me. I find myself in different spheres. Only the sudden onset of the rain prevents me from floating away. First there are single small drops, and then all the clouds over New York seem to descend upon us at once.

The cloud burst announces itself with a clap of thunder and, for a short moment, it is bright as day. Laughing, we run to the intersection and find a shelter that brings some protection. Hardly do we get under this tiny roof and Danny looses no time in embracing me. I can't believe it. Where is my wall? My protection against third degree injuries?

A yellow vehicle approaches again. Danny runs into the street and lifts his arm.

"Taxi!" he calls out into the rain.

The taxi drives up and Danny opens the back door. Quickly I come out from under the roof and jump in the car. Danny follows and slams the door. Before I can say anything, he gives the driver an address that is not mine. The rain drops are pelting loudly on the roof, as if they were going to shoot through the ceiling. But I know they won't make it. So I can feel safe. All the same, something is unsettling me.

"Where are we going?" I ask nervously. My fingers are fidgeting restlessly in my lap.

"Let yourself be surprised," Danny answers slyly.

Somewhat tensed up, I give in to Danny's embrace, which has become almost natural. My light heartedness, which overpowered me, is melting with each mile we ride into the unknown. I don't like surprises. Certainly not when I don't know about them. Now I am irritated that I didn't block Danny's advances from the beginning. Until now, I have fared well with allowing no more relationships in my life. I had five years free of complications. No compromises and no hurt. Why do I need a man in my life? The last time, it cost me my best friend and the life I was used to. Who wants to pay such a high price for a little happiness? And anyway … what am I supposed to do with a rock star? I am completely unmusical. The only instrument I can play is a triangle. So what would I do with a rock star? And what would he do with me?

"Please stop immediately!" I call out to the taxi driver.

"Pardon?" Danny says with amazement. "That's out of the question. Keep going."

"Stop!" I try again.

"Don't listen to her. She doesn't know what she wants."

Certainly I know that! Or don't I? In any case, I've known it for the last few years. Why shouldn't it be that way now? Do I really want something deep within that is different from what I want?

"Then please tell me on the spot where we are going," I tell Danny firmly.

"We're going to my place," he answers my question reluctantly, apparently to calm me down.

Wait a minute. That's a little too fast for me. Or am I interpreting more into this than necessary? Couldn't it be that Danny just wants to show me his guitar collection? Why am I suddenly reluctant about his being close? I was just enjoying it. I'm building a wall around myself again. If something doesn't happen soon, I'm finished before we have even reached his "my place". As if Danny could read my thoughts, he moves closer, pulling me toward him by the shoulders.

"You are a puzzle. Most fans would give a lot to trade places with you. I'm not going to do anything."

Yes you are. You have done something. Broken through my protective wall. I'd like to know why I allowed it to happen. Well, I really couldn't do anything to stop it. It just happened.

We ride for half an eternity through streets unknown to me. Since eighty percent of New York streets are unfamiliar to me, this is not unusual. In a quiet residential area almost on the edge of town, the taxi stops in front of an impressive home. Danny hands the driver a bill and gets out. Skeptical, I sit in the car and marvel wide-eyed at this enormous residence.

"Get out!" Danny says and waits for me impatiently. I give in to the situation and crawl out of the vehicle. Danny grabs my hand and leads me through a gate, which opens for us as if by magic and closes again immediately. In his other hand, I can make out something like a remote. A front yard, as big as a soccer field, is lit up and offers a view of beautifully laid out flower beds. Not far from us, dogs are barking. On a leash. It's better that way. Better not get too close to them. I did grow up with dogs. But these barkers are of a completely different caliber. The house we are approaching is as big as the village where I grew up. Nice shack. It's certainly too big for one person. I wouldn't know what to do with so much space. A little apartment is enough for me. After all, I don't want to "reside" but just live there.

We stride through the entrance, which has to be unlocked with a code, and find ourselves inside the dwelling. Wow! Classy! Everything only the finest. Marble on the walls and on the floor. The furniture was probably as expensive as the house, and the fireplace is big enough for three Santa's to fit through. I am impressed.

But it's not my world. Never would I feel comfortable in this splendid house. Actually, I had imagined his home much differently. More individuality. A little more personality. There might be some photos on the wall or collections of different cultural objects. For instance, things that reveal a bit more about his background. I still don't know of what heritage he is. Or is he blended like me?

"Would you like something to drink?" Danny asks, while he casually flings his shoes in the corner.

"If it's not too far to the kitchen, gladly."

Danny looks at me as if I had spoken a different language than he speaks. Maybe I should try again in Greenlandic?

"Well, don't you like my modest home? You would be the first one."

Why, how many have there been?

Unconsciously, I judge the possibilities for flight. It becomes clear that I am in a fortress and flight is almost out of the question.

"Yes," I respond, "it is perhaps a little large. It's a bit impersonal and without a soul."

"Ha, since when does a house have a soul?"

"It has as much soul as the inhabitant provides it. But this house is unexpressive," I reply to his derisive question.

"So this house is unexpressive." Danny moves in my direction, as if he had forgotten that he wanted to bring me something to drink from the far-away kitchen. "How, in your opinion, do you give a seven million dollar villa expression? Huh? And why is that necessary?"

He folds his arms in front of his body and remains standing in front of me. I look at him as if I had not understood his question. I really didn't. It is clear how you provide a house with a soul. At least for me.

"You share your personality with the house. A home should be a place where you can find peace and strength, if you are no longer in harmony with yourself."

Danny's dimples deepen into a powerful glacier crevasse.

"I don't understand a word."

What is there not to understand?

"Your house is perfect. As beautiful to look at as a photo from a glossy magazine for a furniture outfit. But it's nothing more."

Danny laughs haughtily.

"It doesn't have to be any more. I use it as a place to sleep. Most of the time, I am on the go."

"A rather modest place to sleep. Apparently the demands grow with the fortune."

While I say this, I turn around and take in the exaggerated luxury a second time.

"Why are you being so snippy? Sure it's that way. It would be the same for you, if you didn't know anything more sensible to do with your money."

"Most certainly not. By no means. I would make my money available for charitable purposes, if I had no other reasonable use for it," I counter immediately.

Thanks to the success of my books, I am not completely without means, but I would never have dreamed of acquiring useless living space. Much less surround myself with things whose individual value could compete with a small car.

My parents taught me not to measure the quality of life by material goods, but to find the joy of life in watching a sunset, a flower blooming, or in the mere awareness of one's own existence. My philosophy of life is a very different one. Money only plays a subordinate role in my life.

"You are succeeding in talking me into a bad conscience just because I live like I live. At your delicate age, you have to hold such unrealistic views. But that will change. Show me a wealthy person on this planet, who willingly lives in a hovel, so as not to be untrue to his ideals."

"That is my attitude toward life and no changeable opinion. It is certain that nothing of that will change. Not even if I were to become filthy rich."

Danny's persistent smile about my way of viewing things makes me feel he thinks I am naive. Soon I will feel like a nineteen year old.

"Now I'll get you something to drink. You may drink alcohol or should we first ask your parents for permission?"

You can spare me your dumb observations.

"Thanks, but I don't drink alcohol. I prefer to know what I am saying."

"Is that also one of your many attitudes toward life?" he asks to provoke me and leaves the room.

Not at all fazed by this, I go to the window, which is as big as the entrance to my apartment, and look into the dark courtyard. Why am I here?

What do I expect from this encounter with Danny? There are parallels between us and yet he is completely different from me. His world is so unreal and not accessible to me. Maybe I am just curious. Would like to know who he really is. But what does he want from me? Why did he bring me to his place? He certainly doesn't want to find out anything about me. He thinks he already knows everything. I don't understand myself. It is clear to me why Danny brought me here. A man in his position, who has everything and gets everything he wants, doesn't just want to talk to me. And I? Do I want to wake up in the morning in a bed in which several women have awakened before? Fall in love with a man who can't even remember my name afterwards? Maybe he doesn't even know it any more. He hasn't said it even one more time.

I am a woman with principles and, should I ever want to fall in love again, then only if there is a prospect of a future. This here would not go beyond a liaison and would be absolutely out of the question. I should go now!

When I turn around, I surprisingly land in Danny's arms, who must have been standing behind me unnoticed. Before I can say anything, I sense his warm lips on mine and freeze from bewilderment. I gasp for air. I try to breath but it doesn't work. My thoughts run astray, as his hand runs down my back. My bodily functions are suspended. Everything is running on standby. I can't seem to return his kiss. I am totally blocked. Like a person with asthma, I wheeze and gasp for oxygen, trying to push him away from me. "What is wrong with you? Do I have to explain how a kiss functions?" he laughs.

What? Now he's interpreting everything wrong again.

"I know very well how you kiss!" I say in my own defense.

"Yeah? And what is preventing you? Should we best wait until you are of age?"

That is the last straw.

"I AM, as I just mentioned, twenty eight and I don't have to tolerate your tactless disrespect for my person any longer. I suggest that I go now."

Irritated, I try to fight my way out of his arms, but his embrace is like being chained.

"Hey, you can really get angry. Did I finally manage to lure you out of your reserve, Malina?"

Bewildered, I give up my resistance. He actually said my name. As if he had read my thoughts before.

"Oh, you still know my name? I wouldn't have thought that you remember such incidentals," I spout off combatively.

What is wrong with me? My normally peaceful nature is getting out of control. I am programmed for attack. One more provocative remark and you'll get the battle you are asking for.

Danny's facial features change and his smile freezes.

"What do you think about me?" he asks, sounding hurt. The change remains unnoticed by me. I'm too busy with my readiness for combat, which is unheard of for me. Recently, I've gotten to know myself from a completely new side. I look at my reflection in a silver vase and go toward it. A distorted face bends toward me. Who am I actually? I would like to throw my principles over board and simply give in to my feelings. He only wants a night? – He can have it!

Surely Lucy would not let it go up in smoke. Tomorrow I'll lead my old life again and he can lead his. Neither would fit into the life of the other; but there is nothing to be said against breaking out once and forgetting who one is and where he belongs. So fine, Danny Greyeyes, I'll play along with your game. My reflection comes to an end and I go to Danny, smiling. But, half way there, the doubts return and I remain standing.

"What's going on in your little head?" Danny asks loudly and goes the other half of the way.

His arms stretch around me and wrap around my hips, while he pushes me toward him. Electrified, I wait for the touch of his lips but he just looks at me with an intense gaze.

"Malina. What a pretty name. Do you also know its meaning?"

I thought you wanted to sleep with me and not talk to me.

"It is the name of my native people's sun god," I answer and hope for a continuation of his passionate moves.

But suddenly Mr. Greyeyes breaks into roaring laughter. Did I say something wrong? What is so funny?

"May I ask what is so amusing?"

With some effort, Danny manages to collect himself and, exhausted, sits down on a chair.

"You are well informed about the fact that my parents were Inuit, but it is incredible that you are selling my heritage as your own," Danny comments skeptically.

Stunned, I stand there and digest the information about Danny Greyeyes, which again reveals an unsuspecting parallel. Is this a coincidence? Hard to believe.

"But it is really true," I try to explain; but I'm interrupted on the spot.

"Distorting the facts seems to be your specialty. First a made up age and then you serve me such lies."

Now I've finally had enough.

"It makes no difference what I tell you about myself, since you don't believe me anyway," I say, expressing my disappointment.

"And what you don't know about me you make up. You think I am a dumb, simple girl and …"

"I don't think you are a dumb, simple girl," he interrupts, indignant. "On the contrary. If I believed that, you wouldn't be here this evening."

No? Now I don't understand anything anymore. Slowly, this is becoming too complicated. I definitely should go. Determined, I go to the chair, on which my handbag is lying, and grab for it. I turn around again on my way to the exit. Danny is still sitting in his chair and looking at me quizzically. What a crazy day!

So, not at all or of course?

I run through the unlit front yard and consider how I can get through the gate at the end of the garden without using a sledge hammer. Unfortunately, I failed to get the remote from Danny and, at the moment, I am faced with an unsolvable task. When I've reached the gate, I hear a soft pitter-patter behind me. A ferocious growl causes me to cringe. Hesitating, I turn around and look into the glowing eyes of a monster.

"Oh, what a sweet lap dog you are. Listen, if you don't do anything to me, I promise to do nothing to you. Agreed? Don't force me to use my knowledge of Kung Fu on you."

Empty threats don't seem to deter him. My knees are wobbling like pudding. Now just don't get nervous. If he notices that, I've had it. Can I take care of a few more greetings before my execution? I greet my mother, my father, my brother, Lucy and the rest of the world. How about a last supper? I mean, am I not entitled to that?

A whistle sounds out. The monster runs away. I breathe a sigh of relief. The tension eases abruptly and a decline in strength sets in. I confiscate a big rock for a place to sit. That was close. For a moment, I had seen myself in a meat display case.

"Hey," Danny whispers in my ear. He had hurried over and is kneeling next to me. You can make out dimples of concern on his forehead in the darkness. Is this distress over me?

"Please come in the house, okay?"

What choice do I have? The walls of Alcatraz are nothing compared to this fortress. The Doberman re-appears and sniffs happily as if we were always the best of friends. Can you spare me your innocent sniffing, you stupid mutt!

Danny takes me by the hand and leads me on a safe path back into the house. His beast follows us to the door and then heads off in another direction. Probably to his dog house, cage or whatever. The main thing is away.

Danny pulls me through the hall to a little room in the lower part of the house. It is a beautiful, very homey room with a desk, some book shelves and many decorative pieces on the walls, which reflect his personality. I had been looking in vain for something like this. Little wood carvings are standing in front of the books on the shelves. Similar to the ones my father produces. I go to one figure and take it in my hand.

"A tupilak. Canadian Inuit art," I observe.

"You seem well-versed," Danny marvels. "What details enable you to see this?"

"The figure was cut from hard stone. That is an eye-catching indication. But the style also reveals something about the origin. It is a roughly structured figure. Typical for the southwest region of Canada."

Danny nods with his head in agreement.

"Interesting. Absolutely correct."

I know.

"My father preferred to make his carvings out of walrus ivory. But the tupilak cuttings from all regions are familiar to me."

"Your father is an artist?" Danny inquires. "How does he get walrus ivory in New York?"

I have to grin.

"He lives right at the source."

"I understand. Apparently, he has good sources for his supplies. Give me his address. I'll visit him in the next few days. Maybe I can buy one piece or the other."

Uh? Visit? In Greenland? Did he really understand me?

Carefully I put the figure back on the shelf.

"My father …" I begin the sentence, but am prevented from talking any more by Danny's index finger, which is now resting on my lips. So, again, I am unable to correct a false assumption on his part.

"Not now," he says softly and caresses my face. "What bright, azure blue eyes. Where do they come from?"

Hm.

"From my mother."

Like everything else.

Our faces slowly get closer to each other. His warm breath touches my nose. Hesitantly, our lips meet. He envelops my mouth with his and our tongues begin to play with each other sensually. There is not a trace of blocking now. I am supple like a jelly bean and submit to his kiss. My reservations are blown away. Nothing more is of importance, only Danny and I, his affection, his kisses … until the phone ruins everything.

Irritated, Danny looks at his watch.

"Who can that be at this hour? Sorry, I'll be right back. Don't move and, above all, don't run away again."

He goes to the phone and takes the receiver. Softly, I sneak behind him. An Adam is on the phone. It's his manager. During the conversation, Danny's good mood is transformed into anger. With this facial expression, he could compete with his monster in the garden. He becomes increasingly silent until he doesn't respond at all and hangs up the receiver.

His face muscles twitch and suggest that an explosion is imminent.

What does this mean? What movie is showing? I want to have a say as well.

"It would be better if you go now."

What? Suddenly I'm supposed to go? Just go? Without any explanation?

"May I ask why?" I follow up.

Danny laughs; he sounds embittered.

"You should know that best yourself."

I know nothing at all. This sudden change in weather is too much for me. What kind of scene change is taking place here?

"Sorry, I am completely clueless."

"Save me any further lies and go!"

I am astounded by this insinuation.

"Good, I will go. But first I have the right to know what supposed lies are involved here. Regardless of what your Adam has said about me, you should also hear my side."

Intensely, I ponder what Mr. Adam Fox would have to report about a nondescript person like me. I'm almost a little flattered.

"You are Malina Bergstroem."

Yes and?

"A known book author."

We haven't talked about it, but no lie in sight.

"Your books have to do with Indian tribes."

A trivial way to express it, but you could say that.

"And now I am the object of your studies? You pretended to be a fan. Led me to believe you were somebody else."

I didn't do that one single time.

"What do you want to know about me, huh? Do you want to write a book about me and make a lot of money? Is that what you wanted? The winner of the dinner was actually another person. How much did you pay her for it?"

I recognize how pointless it would be to defend myself. This person seems to judge at a fast speed and misses no opportunity to harm himself with it.

"You don't want to hear the truth at all," and now I take the floor. "It suited you to make a naïve teenybopper out of me. I would like to have told more about myself, but you already had a pigeon hole prepared for me."

I look around and search for my hand bag, since I intend to go on the spot.

"You had all the time in the world to tell me who you are," Danny replies in his unforgiving way.

My handbag is on the telephone stand next to Danny. Crap! There of all places. I certainly did not want to get too close to the wolf in sheep's clothing. Won't help. I'm not going without my equipment. I dash toward Danny and grab my belongings. As I try to slip by him, he places himself in my way.

"You disappointed me," he says softly.

If somebody here has the right to be disappointed, it is me.

"People in your situation draw premature conclusions faster than others. I am sorry for you. How do you succeed in building up friendships?"

Okay, it wasn't exactly my place to ask that. But I take nothing back. My feelings were hurt, so something easily slips out that I might later regret. But not at this moment. That's why I'm not taking it back.

"Don't worry. I have enough friends."

Doesn't matter to me how many friends you have.

Obstinately, I dart past him. At the door, I remain standing again and turn around. Danny is still in the same place and bending his torso in my direction. Too bad it all had to end this way.

"I didn't pretend anything to you. The woman you met today – that is me. And, if you knew my books, you would know that it is nutty to think I had wanted to write one about you. I am an ethnologist and not a gossip columnist."

Looking downward, I leave the room and go.

As I reach the gate in the moonlight, it opens by itself. Above the entrance, I notice a camera has been installed. I consider waving. But then I stop myself. This day was really an educational one. I go home convinced of being more content without a man. Half way more content. And yet the other half longs for more. But, on this evening, the half thought can be declared meaningless. Maybe I can come back to it later. Much later. First, the disappointment over Danny has to be digested. This pain in the stomach area. I am going in some direction. Again, I don't know where I am. It is very good that the evening ended this way. If I am honest, I wouldn't have been able to just check off a one night stand on my sparse spiritual list of experiences with men. The only recorded episode lies some years back and it had led to considerable fractures of my sensitive soul. Of course, I would like to have been more casual in matters of love. But I am not. I talked myself into believing that a night of love could please me and I could simply forget it again. But I couldn't. Good that the evening ended this way. Very good.

At a fork, I stop and consider which of the three possible directions would be the right one.

That doesn't matter. I must reflect on other things. Lost in thought, I simply go straight ahead.

What a crazy thought that I would want to write a book about Danny. That interesting you are not, Danny Greyeyes. A book about a rock star. This idea would never occur to me, even if he were a tribal chief.

My teeth are chattering so much that I am afraid they could crack. Had I known ahead what was awaiting me this day, I would have stayed at home or at least thought of a jacket. Now I only have one single modest wish: a taxi.

Hardly have I made my wish and a yellow car actually turns into the street. I'd like to know how a taxi could stray into this God-forsaken area. It's fine with me. Relieved, I hail the vehicle.

"Where to, young lady?"

I tell the driver my address and look out the window apathetically the rest of the trip. The street lights roll by me like filaments. I see nothing and just stare into space.

"You are lucky, Miss, that I found you in this labyrinth of streets. Why didn't you wait for me in front of the house?"

What is he talking about?

"I don't exactly understand. Weren't you there by chance?"

"Do you seriously believe I'm driving around in this lonely area for fun?"

No, I couldn't imagine that either. So it's not all the same to Danny how I get home. Thanks,

Danny Greyeyes. But that doesn't make up for your behavior just now. I don't answer the taxi driver any more, since I don't want any conversation. Only immerse myself in thought and look out the window. What a day!

Who was the guy?

The next morning the piercing ring at the front door hurls me out of bed. With eyes glued, I look at the alarm. Already ten thirty. I really hadn't intended to sleep half the morning, in spite of the previous short night. My relentless carousel of thoughts last evening kept me from finding any sleep.

Awkwardly, I climb out of bed and throw over my robe. As I open the door, a yawn is stuck in my throat. Danny Greyeyes in person is standing at the door and greets me by holding a newspaper in front of my nose.

"Here!" Friendly as he is, he throws it before my feet. "Is that what you wanted? More publicity for you and your new book?"

Somewhat irritated over this attack and his uncultivated behavior, plus the idea of encountering Danny in my robe at my front door, I bend down for the paper, without a word. I try not to think about how Danny might have gotten my address and what prompted him to visit me personally.

"You don't need to turn the pages. It's right on the front page," he snaps at me. Hesitating, I unfold the newspaper and shudder as my own face, next to Danny's jumps out at me, almost life size. The headline under this gigantic photo shocks me even more.

"The lady's man and the publicity shy author now a couple."

Then they know more than I. How can Danny assume I would have wanted that? I'm happy when I can read my name as seldom as possible.

"You did a fine job of inventing that one," he accuses me again.

I only wonder what would bother him so, if that had been my intention. It shouldn't matter to him if I gained some advantage from meeting with him. In any case, it would be no disadvantage to him. So where is the problem, Danny Greyeyes? The only person who has one now is me. So much attention to my person is quite annoying.

"Thanks for coming by personally to take care of this. Can I help you in some other way?" I ask cautiously and close the door a bit, with the intention of letting go any moment. I don't think I would like to put up with his gruff manner any longer.

Unexpectedly, Danny puts his foot in the doorway and forces his way into the apartment. Hey, hey, that is going way too far. His unrestrained entry into my four walls could amount to a criminal "infringement" or something like that. You could say trespassing. So I am entitled to scream.

"Why you? Explain it to me please. How can you, as meek as a lamb, be so crafty? How could I deceive myself this way?"

Before I can reply, the door is pushed open from outside and my brother Namid is standing on the threshold, ready for battle.

"Hey, you thug," he says turning directly to Danny, "See that you scram and keep your hands off my sister!"

Certainly it would be better to clear up the situation directly, but no explanation occurs to me in all the confusion. What sort of situation is it? A robbery can be ruled out and a rape is not so disciplined. I have all my clothes on, and it surely wouldn't have come to a removal of these.

Danny looks aghast at my brother, who lets his chest bulge out in a threatening pose. Namid can't know that Danny is possibly harmless. And yet can I be certain? His anger seems somewhat unrestrained. So it wouldn't be a bad idea to ban him from my chambers. I'd only like to know why Danny doesn't just forget me, like all the women in his life. Why does he turn up here today? Who am I that I would be worthy of a second encounter with a rock star?

"Come on! Get out of here!" Namid demands a second time. Danny looks back and forth between Namid and me.

"That is your brother?" he asks, perplexed.

Yes, and I am extremely happy that he exists. As long as I can remember, he has fearlessly involved himself in all the conflicts that affected me and heroically stood at my side. Somehow the role of the big brother suits him. Only I'm not certain whether I need to be rescued at this moment.

Before Namid gets the opportunity to let his proven fists speak for themselves, Danny makes a quiet retreat. Unfortunately, I can't tell what sort of expression is on his face. That would have been a crucial hint about his mindset. Why that is suddenly so important to me isn't exactly clear.

"Who was that? What did the guy want from you? And what did I read about you in the paper today?" Namid asks, while he looks for a comfortable spot on the sofa.

"Oh, you've already read it also?" I ask anxiously. Knowing well that there will hardly be a person who is not informed about what I myself didn't know until now. Namely, all of a sudden being "a pair" with Danny Greyeyes.

Namid puts his legs on the table and lights a cigarette. It's never interested him that this apartment is inhabited by non-smokers. I go into the kitchen and look for an ashtray but can't find one. So I put an empty fish can in front of his feet.

Straight faced, Namid grabs the fish can and accepts it as a substitute for an ashtray. I turn up my nose.

"What does all of this mean? I know you, little sister. Not on your life would you ever waste your time on such a guy."

Embarrassed, I cover my face with my right hand and look listlessly at the floor. The runner with crumbs on it reminds me of my domestic duties.

Not on my life would I … with such a guy? Maybe he also meant not on my life would I … with a guy at all? He knows well that I have lived almost in celibacy the last few years. So this headline must seem absurd to him.

"Actually, it means nothing. That is, I don't know exactly what it means. I just learned about it from Danny."

My brother freezes into a statue.

"That guy was Danny Greyeyes? Why didn't you say anything?"

Yes, quite right. Why did I say nothing?

"I don't know. The sudden appearance of you and Danny and my picture in the newspaper – I was completely confused."

There is a hiss as Namid puts out his cigarette in the remains of the fish sauce. He leans forward to put the supposed ash tray on the table. His long black hair falls and swings before his shoulders.

"Are you together or not?" he asks with interest.

"No … or maybe … really not. No idea."

Why is he asking such difficult questions? If I only knew myself. In any case, we are not together. I would characterize it as a mistake hardly worth mentioning, with a rough phase of reflection, which led to a premature end of the budding romance. Short little romance with and without consequences. Yes, you could put it that way.

"What then?" Namid asks. "Did I make a fool of myself? Is something going on between you two or not?"

"Nothing more. Naturally I mean nothing, without 'more'. Don't worry! It was only a mistake. Nothing else."

I twist the belt of my robe around my finger and look out the window. Namid gets up from the couch and pours himself a glass of water in the kitchen.

"Too bad," he comments tersely.

Too bad? It's better I don't ask how he means that. For I can imagine. Namid doesn't miss out on anything. He changes his women like other people do their underwear. My life must seem very bleak to him. And yet I am an extremely content person.

Men only create problems. Hardly do I get to know one and my whole life is turned upside down. Emotional chaos, a "sleepless night without sleep" and my picture in a local tabloid. That is suggestive of further trouble. My familiar tranquility will melt like ice cream in the sun.

It's Lucy's fault. Yes, exactly. If it hadn't been for Lucy, this meeting with Danny would never have taken place. Best friends are risky. I knew it. Only Lucy didn't snatch away a man but, instead, she found one. Nonetheless, it is difficult to declare her guilty on all counts. I can't rule out the possibility that I bear a large part of the responsibility for this misery myself. Why did I get myself into this mess? Why did I go to Danny's? These are indications of a certain amount of personal negligence.

"You don't love him, do you?" Namid asks unexpectedly.

So this question clearly goes too far. How could I love a man after such a short warming phase? Before I fall in love, the North Pole will have to be free of ice. Practically speaking, I am the North Pole.

"I don't know," I hear myself answer.

That wasn't me. I would never say something like that. I don't know would mean that I don't rule out the idea that dormant feelings are budding out. That is impossible. I'm sure of that.

"In case you need my help, you know where you can find me, little sister."

Actually, I never know that exactly. But, as a rule, Namid is always there as soon as I experience the smallest amount of distress. He seems to sense that.

"Yes, thanks, but I'll manage. I think so. I always have. Why should it be different now? Anyway, thanks a lot. I just have to sort out some things. My feelings, my life. But I'll manage somehow. I have to."

What sort of babbling is that?

Namid comes over to me and wraps his protective arms around me.

"You're a little rattled. Would you like to talk about it?"

I would like to, but about what exactly? That I feel hurt and Danny Greyeyes has made a calculating killer lady out of me?

Or should I talk about my confusing feelings, which are causing me worry? I could use a trash can. But, as a rule, aren't best friends there for garbage disposal? Good, Namid is my brother, but he is also a man. And men would certainly never betray their sex. But maybe they would make an exception for their own sister. However, can I be certain?

"Maybe later. If I need your advice, I'll be standing on your door mat. You can count on that."

"That is typical for you," Namid reproaches me. "Why do you always think it would be better to decide everything yourself? After the separation from Phil, you didn't say a word about your heartache."

Phil. I haven't heard this name for five years, much less spoken it. I choke the minute I hear the name pronounced.

I consider it unnecessary to burden other people with my problems. The best method of forgetting is not to think about it anymore. And so that you don't think about it, you just don't talk about it anymore. It's as simple as that. I've always done well with this. What's wrong with it?

"You are right," I capitulate. "But, believe me, I'm okay."

Namid nods his head. He fishes in his wallet for his business card and puts it on the table.

"I've moved again. My new address."

Namid moves around like a vagabond. If he ever does settle down, it will be on account of a woman. That woman he has not found up until now.

After saying good-bye to Namid, I try to shed my thoughts with a shower. The pleasure of the warm shower only lasts a short time, until the persistent ringing of the phone causes me to hurry out of the bathroom.

My publisher is on the phone. What is causing this abnormal behavior? We hardly talk to each other. Most things are clarified in writing. In the case there is something to clarify.

"Miss Bergstroem, is that you?" he asks uncertainly. No wonder, since my voice is largely unknown to him. I have to listen closely to recognize myself. When do I hear myself talking?

"Yes." Short and snappy. I most like to answer this way.

"Good. Listen, Miss Bergstroem, I just read it in the newspaper."

Let me guess. No, I'll never figure it out myself. Tell me.

"Yes?"

"You know, your private life is none of my business ..."

Right, it is none of your business at all. Only mine and mine alone. Otherwise nobody else.

"… it is only that: This increasing public interest in your person could prove useful. What I want to say is: We should move up the publication date of your next book and arrange public appearances as soon as possible. What do you think of that, Miss Bergstroem?"

What I think of it?! Nothing and, again, nothing! No way! Ditch the book! Anything, but no public appearances!

"Of course I am aware that you don't want too much ado about your person. So we could make the book signings as short as possible. Let's say, maybe one hour a day."

Per day? And how many days are involved?

"I've already spoken with the printer's. There is no reason not to start distribution of the book next month."

So you organize everything behind my back and then let me know. Then I only need to say "yes". For a "no" is no longer possible. I love having the choice. Especially when the decision is already definite. Then the choice is not so hard. I call that self-determination.

"Yes, so …," I ponder a bit loudly.

"So you agree. That is wonderful. I've already been plugging it in the book stores. At three o'clock on Wednesday in four weeks, there will be a signing at the Hamilton bookstore. I'll send you information on other appointments."

"Then how many are there?" I ask in a worried tone.

"Oh, don't worry, ha, ha, not all of them are set, ha, ha, but I don't want to expect more than five or six from you, ha, ha."

Five or six. So many! *One* appointment is an unreasonable demand. But five or six is murder.

After the call, I slide to the floor like a limp little Michelin man.

What am I going to do now? The decision was already made for me. I desperately need help in saying no. That could simplify my life greatly.

"No! No! No, no …! No, no, no, no …"

It's very simple. Why doesn't that work, when it depends on that?

Five to six promotional gigs for the new book. Danny's false assumptions about my intentions are encountering fertile ground.

Right into the midst of the catastrophe!

"Lucy! It is completely impossible for me to go into this bookstore. What I am supposed to do there? Why do the books have to be signed? I don't know how I'm supposed to get there. My car won't start. I'm sure it won't start. It won't attract their attention if I don't show up."

I go into my room and plop onto the bed, not even noticing the beautiful weather. My stage fright is ruining all perceptive faculties. Lucy comes in and sits on the bed next to me.

"You can handle it. Just look through the people! You don't need to look directly at them."

No, I don't need to do that. But I always look carefully at all people.

What's worse is that they will definitely stare at me. Every single one of them. They will gape and stare right through me. I hate that! Am I a painting? I don't want to be stared at.

"What if they are not interested in my book but only in the romance with Danny?"

"Hey, that's all the same to you. Forget this Danny once and for all!"

"I would like to. Unfortunately, for the last four weeks, I've had to read a rumor about him and me almost every day. Yet I haven't seen him any more at all."

Lucy gets up and pulls on my sleeve.

"What does that matter? You're going to this book store now! I will drive you there personally, so that you do show up."

She smiles at me as if she were pleased by my suffering. What sort of sadistic streak is lurking in her? I surrender and stand up. She is right. A friend who is right can be useful, but also uncomfortable. It would be easier to have a nap and, afterwards, attend the signing live in front of the television. Why do I have to go there in person?

Lucy explains to me on the trip to the book store why I could never watch myself live on television from home. I had already thought that and didn't want to know so much in detail; but Lucy takes her job as a friend rather seriously. In no case would she allow my IQ to be harmed by such an absurd hypotheses.

As we reach the book store, I notice the crowds of people in front of the entrance. There is a lot of hustle and bustle so the streets are congested. Cars parking on the street line up on top of each other. Everything is dense. It seems like half the city has gathered in front of the book store.

Lucy! Full turning maneuver. Turn off! We're sailing toward home.

"We're not going to get through here," Lucy determines. "My goodness, what is going on here?!"

See, Lucy, I should have stayed at home. In bed. Before the television. The alternative is a big threat.

"Maybe you should get out here and walk the last bit."

"Pardon?! You can't be serious. The crowd will tear me into little shreds before I have reached my goal. I won't arrive in one piece."

Not a sensible idea.

"Please stop here! I have to think," I tell Lucy.

She does what I say.

My thumbs are turning around at the speed of light. It's hard to think with the sight of this horde of people.

Back entrance. That worked once. Lucy looks restlessly at her watch. This blocks my attempt at thinking. Does this have to be? I know myself that time is getting short. That does me no good. Models for a solution are desperately sought.

"I'm going to walk," I tell Lucy.

I open the car door and jump out. Before I let the door close, I bend forward.

"Oh, Lucy, if I don't show up by this evening, then you must convey the sad news of my premature demise to my parents. They will certainly understand."

Lucy smiles as if in distress.

"I'll cross my fingers for you."

Yes, that will help for sure. Cross them all!

Boldly, I go along the middle median and consider switching to the sidewalk. What do I do if they zoom at me like a swarm of mosquitoes? Maybe they won't recognize me.

The arm of a man far away is pointing at me. Like in a game of dominoes, those behind him raise their arms, one after another. The swarm of mosquitoes takes off. An approximately infinite number of human mosquitoes merge into a marching formation for the attack. Panic stricken, I look around for alternate routes. Too late. Soon they will have reached me. Like a horde of escaped lunatics, they are calling out and waving. Their speed is increasing. If something doesn't occur to me, I am dead.

A large dark car stops next to me and the tires squeak. The back door is pulled open from within and a firm grip suddenly pulls me from the median into the car's interior.

"Damn! Get away from the street right now!"

The door slams and the car quickly moves back. I slide into the foot well of the car and bump my head.

Before I can find an explanation for the unexpected turn of my life-threatening situation, I am lifted into the seat by the arms. Dazed, I look to the side and recognize Danny Greyeyes next to me. At the steering wheel a shady man unknown to me. Have I missed something?

"Have you taken leave of your senses? They've been waiting for you like blowflies for hours. Do you want to let them tear you to pieces?

You must realize that you can't just simply walk in there."

Well, yes, there is something true to that. I still don't understand anything anymore.

"Is that a coincidence that you are here?" I ask bewildered.

Danny gives his driver a sign that I don't know how to interpret.

"Of course not. I will drop you off at the back entrance of the book store and wait for you."

"You want to wait for me? But why?" Here a chapter has gotten by me. Why is Danny here? And why does he want to wait for me?

"It's because I don't want you to get in trouble again. It's just not clear to you what it means to be prominent."

No, naturally not. Since I'm not prominent. I am only me. As insignificant as a house fly.

"I don't need to be protected. I can look out for myself."

We reach the book store "from behind".

"I saw that. You seem to have no idea what is awaiting you there. People are just waiting for a mistake from you to satisfy their craving for sensation. You just don't understand what it means to be my girlfriend."

Did I hear the words "my girlfriend"? Or is what I am hearing a Fata Morgana? If you can hear something like that.

"I am not your girlfriend!"

What an imagination he has! Outrageous.

"Then read the paper! It can't have escaped you that they all presume that. This fact alone makes you terribly interesting to them."

Don't imagine too much!

"Do you mean to say that usually nobody is interested in me?"

"No, that is not what I mean. You're twisting the facts." The car stops at the "back door". "Damn! Why don't you want to understand me?"

If it were just a matter of not wanting to understand him, we would be a step further. It is simply incomprehensible to me what Danny's sudden appearance on the scene means. I haven't heard anything from him for a good four weeks. And now he simply picks me up from the median and tells me that one becomes more significant as his girlfriend and should not go through the front entrance of a book store, although I am not his girlfriend and did not intend to use the store's front entrance but just headed for it.

Doesn't matter; I have to go in now.

I try frantically to open the car door, but Danny prevents me from doing it.

"Malina, wait a moment."

Danny bends down somewhat to me, so that his breath envelopes me.

"Do you really think that you'll manage in there?" he asks, showing his reservations, and looks at me tensely, showing off those dimples.

I nod my head and wonder about his concern. Why this sudden change of heart? What is different today from four weeks ago? I don't find the answer in the few seconds available. Silently I open the car door and get out. No time remains to look back again. Mr. Hamilton, the book store in person, comes running toward me.

"Miss Bergstroem, finally! We were worried about you. It's good that you found the back entrance. We had no idea what a huge rush was awaiting us here. Please come on!"

Rushing about, Mr. Hamilton runs ahead of me and points out the way. Why do I suddenly sense such calm within me? Where is my uncertainty? I want my stage fright back. I'm used to it.

"We have prepared a small stage for you. Fortunately, the audio engineering is working again. An hour ago, it went on the blink. Everything was malfunctioning. No sound, no light. But now everything is ready for you."

My agitation returns. I'm supposed to talk to the people under a spotlight on a stage? Nobody said anything about that. I am not prepared for speaking. And I'm a slouch at improvising.

Mr. Hamilton remains standing.

"Please wait here a moment! I will announce you and then call you on stage. Do you have a pen for the signing afterwards?"

Listlessly, I shake my head.

"Here, take mine!"

He pushes his pen in my hand. What is happening here? Why am I not the least bit aware of the procedure today? My publisher assured me that it was a matter of a "silent" book signing.

"So, I'll get started," Mr. Hamilton comments and steps onto the little stage set up on the sales floor.

I hardly hear his words about me and the book. Questions rattle around in my head. What is Danny doing here? Why is he waiting for me outside? Why in God's name wasn't I informed that I am supposed to give a talk today? What should I do?

Mr. Hamilton calls me onto the stage. The applause of the audience penetrates my ear like an echo from afar. It seems like the cutting of a scythe. Death is waiting for me out there. My legs start to move. All on their own. How does that happen? I see a black tunnel and move toward the spotlight. Mr. Hamilton turns over the microphone. It feels like a stove pipe. Does Mr. Hamilton have fever? The light gets brighter.

Dying must be like this, I think. The scythe seems polished. The echo from the world beyond fades away. Something must occur to me fast. The looks of the visitors shoot through my body like pellets. Desperately, I search for words in my head.

But I only find a big black hole, which devours everything that comes near it. My memories, my hard-earned knowledge, words of every type have disappeared. It's no use. Even if I wanted to, I couldn't utter more than one or two vowels.

I decide to put the microphone on the table in front of me and just take off. But, before I can, the microphone is skillfully removed from my hand. Enthusiastic calls and applause resound through the room. The click of countless cameras is like hundreds of little glass marbles, which are falling on the ground. There is a flurry of camera flashes from all sides. Suddenly, Danny is next to me. He smiles while he puts his arms around my shoulders. Some of the girls shriek and hop like wild chickens, trying to jump on the stage. What an insane asylum! Where am I? What am I doing here? What is Danny doing here?

"Thank you!" Danny yells into the microphone. "Thanks for this reception. But I am not the main guest today, but rather my charming girlfriend Malina Bergstroem. Her new book, which she would like to introduce to you today, is about a people known to be one of the oldest on earth. The aborigines. This book vividly conveys the deplorable state of affairs of Australia's natives and how their world was shaken by the arrival of the Europeans. She lived there for several months with a tribe, to learn about its customs, rituals, and conventions. I think it is a really successful and suspenseful report. I am convinced that you will like it as well as I do."

Thunderous applause.

Surprised, I look at Danny. He read my book?

Mr. Hamilton again dashes onto the stage and squeezes Danny's hand.

"My goodness, Mr. Greyeyes, that is a surprise. Would you be so kind and sign a few autographs with Miss Bergstroem? That is sensational that I have you together here on the stage. I hope you don't mind if the press takes a few pictures of you both?"

Danny looks at me.

"As far as I'm concerned, but please don't forget the real cause of this event. It's important that the book stands in the foreground."

"Of course," Mr. Hamilton assures us and invites the audience onto the stage for the signing.

Quickly I use the opportunity to ask Danny a question.

"Why?" I ask tersely.

Another formulation of my pressing question doesn't occur to me and, besides, this strikes the core of my intellectual confusion rather well. With "why?" I am basically covering all the questions shooting through my head at once. Danny's satisfied smile hits me in the face. Was that his answer? Somehow I hoped for a more meaningful answer. People are rushing at Danny and me. I pull out my pen and sign everything handed me. Mostly books. But now and again, arms, hands, and T-shirts. Over and over, cameras are aimed at us and pictures snapped. I feel uncomfortable in this crowd and notice how the first beads of sweat are forming on my forehead. Inconspicuously, I squint at my watch and, getting depressed, realize that the hour signing has run over into the "second hour" signing.

My prevalent feeling of warmth could be because I am almost a born seal and thus like it cool. But I won't rule out the possibility that my anxiety is allowing my metabolism to warm up. If my circulation should want to grab a quick break, it would be helpful to have a sign ahead of time. To explore the situation, I take a quick look at the crowd, in the hope that the line will soon break up.

Unfortunately, I determine with dismay that more masses of people are moving up. A drop of sweat falls from my forehead and splashes on my hand. The spotlight is reflected in the liquid. It would certainly be advisable to break up as long as my circulation is still "circulating". Next to me, Danny doggedly scribbles one autograph after the next. I pinch my eyes together and try to sharpen my blurred field of vision. My legs are trembling like guitar strings that have been struck. Now something is going to happen. The floor under me begins to sway. My hand grabs Danny's arm; he is standing right next to me. He seems to understand.

"So, people, that was it for today."

Long faces. A grumbling sounds through the room. Don't care. Have to get out of here fast.

I try yet another departing gesture and clear the field with marching steps, past Danny, past

Mr. Hamilton, past any shelves, until my legs won't carry me anymore and bend like straws. Everything is black and I lose consciousness.

No idea how long I laid around that way. Between the shelves. But now something is happening with my circulation. When I open my eyes, fast little dots are romping around in my field of vision.

Can somebody sharpen the image?

"For heaven sake, Miss Bergstroem, are you okay?" This voice belongs to Mr. Hamilton. It's supposed to be a joke. If I were okay, I wouldn't be lying between his shelves. The dots are slowly going away and I recognize Danny over me. With his dimpled look, he kneels next to me and strokes my head.

"So," he comments gently.

So … here I am again. You are welcome to caress my head for a while. I like that.

"Are you doing better now?" he asks.

No, far from it. About an hour of head stroking from being better. Or longer.

Unfortunately, I nod my head. I have to practice that with the right motor activity at the decisive moment.

Danny helps me up. Mr. Hamilton makes a distraught impression.

"Miss Bergstroem, I am so sorry. Had I known that you … How should I express myself …? Your publisher tried to dissuade me … from organizing such a big event. He pointed out that you … well, are somewhat uptight at public appearances. But I couldn't anticipate ..."

So Mr. Hamilton created this mess for me. Well, thank you very much.

"You're not serious?" Danny asks indignantly. "Malina was not informed about today's procedure? You simply let her walk into a trap? Just to get your store full?"

Hey, it is my job to get irritated about this. What do you have to do with it? I find it nice of you, but why? Yes, exactly! We haven't clarified the why. It's getting to be time for an explanation.

"I am inconsolable. Really, Mr. Greyeyes."

"Spare yourself the hypocrisy. You are all equally unscrupulous. One is like the other. The main thing is that the money rolls in. This will have consequences for you!" Danny threatens him and pushes me to the exit.

No it won't! It wasn't all that bad. And you have nothing at all to do with it. Why are you getting mixed up in it?

Still feeble, I shuffle to the car. Danny opens the car door for me, and I fall back listlessly onto the seat. Something to eat would not be a bad thing. Again, I had abstained from breakfast since my stomach was not present. What should you do, completely without a stomach? But now it seems to be there again and is calling attention to itself. Did I swallow a dog? Danny seats himself next to me and the sinister driver takes off roughly. My stomach is turning like the drum of a washing machine and causing more nausea.

"I'm feeling queasy," I let Danny know.

He opens all the windows with the push of a button and again strokes my hair. Could be that that will help. More, please.

Was I just nauseated? My thoughts are floating in a vacuum. I think about nothing. When my indisposition finally vanishes, my brain begins to work again. Now I would be interested to know where we are going. Am I being kidnapped?

"Where are we going?" I ask with a subdued voice.

The voice is just as subdued as a voice can be, if one is nauseous, but has forgotten about it, because other circumstances have come to the fore. Circumstances like "caressing the head" or fear of "being kidnapped".

"Wait and see!" is the answer I get.

Where is "wait and see" located?

"But I would like to know!" I say to force the issue. In no case do I simply want to wait for my kidnapping. If I'm to be kidnapped, then I have to know it now.

"There is something I would like to discuss with you."

"Yes?" I ask. What could a Danny Greyeyes have to discuss with me? "You can discuss that with me here."

My goodness, my curiosity was always a great burden. I simply can't repress it. Not even with the greatest of effort.

"We'll be right there and then you will learn about everything," Danny explains to me with a smile.

The car stops in front of a yellow mansion. The gold colored sign on the door reads "Dr. Smith, Attorney at Law".

Wouldn't know what I'm supposed to do at a lawyer's.

"So, we are here."

Danny gets out of the vehicle before me. I climb out behind and look around. Nice area. One mansion after the other. The chimneys on the roof seem like towering noses. Much too exclusive. I grew up in a wooden house of 56 square meters. We had an outhouse and I had to share a room with Namid. I would never feel comfortable in a mansion.

Until now, I never had anything to do with lawyers and don't think that it is necessary. I think I'll get lost now. While Danny approaches the entrance, I remain standing at the polished sign.

"What's with you?" Danny wonders. "Come on!"

Pooh! Why should I? No idea what I'm supposed to do here.

I decide to strike a new path and go home.

"Hey, stop immediately! Where do you want to go?"

"Sorry, but I'm going. I don't like this secretiveness. You don't want to explain anything, so I don't want to go in."

"I didn't know that you were so desperately craving an explanation. Why are you so impatient? If you go in there with me now, your questions will be answered."

Why is he making it so suspenseful? Good, I'll accompany him, but only because he helped me out of a fix before.

"Good, I've thought it over."

How could I say "no"? My speech organ is not designed for this word.

Danny's trusting smile relieves the tense atmosphere between us. Hesitating, I go toward him.

"Thanks," he replies, relieved, and pushes the bell.

The door is opened by a prim lady of middle age, whose smile muscles have been retired for some time. She points the way through a hall that is so gigantic one would think he was in a house or a room. At the end of the hallway, we come upon a large door. We then enter a spacious office. At the window is a desk as big as the loading space of a truck trailer. A portly man in a three-piece suit, no longer appearing so youthful, comes toward us.

"Mr. Greyeyes. Nice of you to stop by. And you are unmistakably the pretty Miss Bergstroem."

He extends his fleshy hand to me.

"Believe me, Miss Bergstroem, I have read all of your books and am a true fan of all your publications."

Oh yes?

"Please sit down. Can I offer you some coffee?"

Danny nods.

"And for you, Miss Bergstroem?"

I don't intend to stay here longer than ten minutes. For this negligible amount of time, I don't need any life-extending refreshments.

"That's very nice but I'm not thirsty. Thank you very much."

Mr. Smith orders two cups of coffee over the intercom.

"Very good," the intercom answers.

"Since you are appearing here together, I assume that Miss Bergstroem agrees with all points and the prepared agreement will be signed today?"

My spine stiffens and forces me into an upright posture. Thunderstruck, I let my gaze wander from Mr. Smith to Danny, who gives me an innocent smile.

Until now, not a single question has been answered. Instead, there are even more questions. What game is being played here?

"What is this about?" I inquire nervously.

My fingers are twirling around each other like crochet needles.

"No, Mr. Smith, that is a misunderstanding," Danny says, taking the floor. "Actually, I just wanted to inform Miss Bergstroem about everything."

Nice. Then out with it!

"I'm dying to know!"

My posture is increasingly tense, as if I had an iron rod in my back. Relaxed, Danny leans back and crosses his legs.

"I'd like for you to write a book about me, Malina."

Thanks. That's enough. You don't need to say any more. Where is the exit?

Exasperated, I get up. Mr. Smith gets up as well.

"Don't trouble yourself, Mr. Smith. I'll find the way out myself. Danny, Mr. Smith, have a nice day."

The coffee is just arriving. How fitting. I go toward it and the server. Baffled, she pulls the tray to her breast to make room in the door frame. Remarkably large door. Two people and two cups of coffee together actually fit through it.

What was Danny Greyeyes imagining? Does he seriously believe I will play his ghost writer? He can compose his memoirs alone.

Loud steps are following me. The parquet floor is vibrating.

"Malina, please wait! Why don't you hear me out?"

Deflated, I remain standing and turn toward him.

"When I saw you last time, you threw a newspaper at my feet. You reproached me for using your prominence to gain more attention for my book. Whatever I said about myself you had to question it. Even my age. By the way, my father is not a wood craftsman in New York. Instead, he lives with my mother in Greenland in a village of 100 souls, where, rather lonely, I grew up with my brother. And I can well understand how discrimination due to skin color feels. That is to say, I have experienced that myself. You think you are something special because you are prominent, and you surely think you can allow yourself everything, ruthlessly hurting the feelings of other people. You can't suddenly burst into my life four weeks later and ignore all these events, acting as if nothing had happened. If you had read just one single one of my books, you'd know that I would never write a biography about another person."

So now I have really vented my feelings. I should do that much more often.

Danny's dimple glance focuses on me. Does this have to happen now? It robs me of all decisiveness. With small steps, he comes toward me and remains standing in front of me.

"Yes, it's true. I am an idiot," Danny ascertains. "I know that now. Actually, I wanted to explain everything to you in peace, but apparently I had no time for it. I am sorry about all of it. You must believe me. I have read all of them. Your books are terrific. Your first one about life in Greenland especially fascinated me. I understand now who you are."

So? I don't know that myself. It could entail certain advantages to know someone who knows me.

"You write with such dedication about the life of other peoples. You succeed in explaining everything so vividly and in reflecting the feelings of people in your texts. You enliven their culture and give them a face that they have lost through the deprivation of their freedom. I'd like for you to put my face in perspective. What is there to say against it, Malina? You mingled with other people to do the research for your books, in order to study them. Now I'm asking you to move in with me for a while, to study me."

I am appalled and my eyes open wide, reaching the size of two extra large eggs. I really don't believe that I just heard something about "moving in" with Danny, but it couldn't hurt to question him.

"You want me to move in with you?"

"Yes. How else do you want to get to know me better? It's important to me that you don't just write what I tell you, but rather what you see of me. Judge me based on your feeling."

"But why would you want that?"

"Because it is important to me that the people out there get to know the right Danny Greyeyes and not his façade or what the media have made of him. I'm convinced you possess the talent to portray people in the right light."

Mr. Smith joins up and gets involved in our conversation.

"Miss Bergstroem, please just come back into the office and look at the agreement more carefully. You'll notice that Mr. Greyeyes took care that everything was formulated fairly and in your favor."

Well fine. I can take a quick look at it. Together, we go into the empty office, in which the coffee has unfolded its flavor. So I recall that I am hungry.

Mr. Smith hands me a three page contract. I accept it and struggle with my doubts. Without having half way filled my stomach, I won't succeed in reading it. Thanks to the hunger setting in, my concentration leaves something to be desired. Straining, I try to read the first paragraph.

What do I do if, out of despair, my stomach digests itself?

My eyes dart over the second paragraph.

Can you live without a stomach?

Third paragraph.

I'd like to know how digestion without a stomach works.

Second page, first paragraph.

Or aren't you hungry anymore?

Second page, second paragraph.

A life without a stomach would have certain advantages.

Second page, third paragraph.

I could eat a lot, without getting full.

Third page, first and second paragraph all at once.

That is working like clockwork. Soon I'll be through.

Last paragraph!

Finished!

What did I actually just read?

"So, what do you say, Miss Bergstroem?"

Hm. Would have to scan it fast again if I were going to say something. I only remember the words "three months". Everything else was just letters strung together. The urgent procurement of some nourishment would be much more important at the moment. Impatiently, I look to the door.

"You can trust me absolutely, Malina. I want everything to transpire honestly between us. In the case that the book is a success, each of us will get his fair share. All the expenses for the coming time together will be mine. Regardless of what kind. Your creature comforts will be taken care of."

Yes, "creature comforts" are the key words. Can I get something to eat now?

Mr. Smith hands me his pen. I take it and play with the push button. Klick … klack … klick … klack.

"Miss Bergstroem, it would be foolish if you don't sign. You will both profit from it."

I nod lost in thought. Why do I nod? No idea what Mr. Smith or Danny have just said to me. Klick … klack. My hunger is affecting my ability to hear. Klick … klack. The only thing I still hear is the angry growling of my stomach.

Danny seems relieved about my definite reaction. With a satisfied smile, he prepares for the signature and pushes the signed pages to me.

"Now only your signature is missing, Miss Bergstroem."

Temporarily, my power of judgment comes into play, and it is clear to me what is involved.

"I still don't quite know if I really want this. I …"

"Miss Bergstroem, I thought we were already beyond this point. Is it clear to you what this could mean for your career?"

Hunger can be very painful. What am I supposed to be clear about? My stomach seems to be pricking with spears against the inside wall.

"Simply sign and don't think too much about it."

If I could only succeed in thinking. My hand leads the pen over the paper, and slowly I scribble my signature next to Danny's.

But, at the same moment, my reason returns. With dismay, I notice what I have just done. I have actually let myself be coaxed and signed this contract. Under normal circumstances, that would never have happened to me at all. I don't have the slightest idea what is written on this paper. Probably I have sold my soul. Oh God! Hand it over! I must tear it up.

Mr. Smith takes the pages. My hands grasp at thin air. Oh no! What have I done?!

"In the coming days I will send you both a copy. I wish you much luck!"

In front of the mansion, the dark car with the shady driver is still waiting for us. Danny goes ahead to open the door for me.

I wouldn't dream of going somewhere with you. I would rather starve than to get into this car again. You obnoxious fraud!

Defiantly, I continue on my way in another direction.

"Good. As you wish. But don't forget! After next week, we will spend the coming three months together. Whether you want to or not."

What? Next week already? For three months? How could I overlook that?

The Moving In

I admit that, for various reasons, I was not very alert on this day. Nonetheless, Lucy did not have to behave so sarcastically toward me when I reported on my calamity. From a friend I expected understanding and comfort. Solidarity, when it depends on that. In my opinion, she had failed miserably in this matter. My efforts to keep her from noticing my humiliation seem to fail. On the day I am to move out, I am sitting on my suitcase and speculating one last time how I can avoid this thing with Danny, without committing a breach of contract.

Lucy knows me well and suspects it is not a good sign when I absolutely don't open my mouth. In the normal case, that is an indication of the blues that I detect. She pulls up a chair and sits across from me and my suitcase.

"Malina, you should try to explain it to Danny. Maybe he'll understand that you can't do that."

I don't answer Lucy. My mouth is as if it were sealed up.

Don't forget that I signed something in a delirium.

Meanwhile, the copy of the contract was sent to me. I could finally read in detail what is awaiting me. In the event that different points are violated, the estimated contract fine would ruin me. Externally, I was in full possession of my mental faculties on this day, so that a challenge of the contract would be completely pointless.

Three months of imprisonment would await me. I will have to spend this time in the limelight of the general public. For the agreement obligates me to accompany Danny to all official events. Then all the newspapers will be convinced of a romantic relationship.

Should I succeed in preventing my premature demise over these three months, I will seek out a quiet place at the North Pole. I will build an igloo and spend the rest of my life self-sufficiently, in absolute seclusion. I don't want anything more. Only my peace.

"Three months will be over fast. Maybe you'll even be sorry when it's over."

What kind of inept observations of Lucy's are those? I will celebrate when the time is over. In case these should be the last three months of my life, it would be advisable to say good-bye to Lucy in a fitting way. We shouldn't depart with any resentment in the air. Maybe we'll never see each other again.

Having reached the greatest insight, I get up from my suitcase to give Lucy a hug.

Take care, you true soul. Good-bye and never forget me!

"I will miss you, Malina. Stay in touch, okay?"

"I will."

Depressed, I grab my suitcase and go.

The taxi drives me to Danny's modest domicile. When we arrive, the taxi driver examines me critically in the rear view mirror.

"Wow, young lady, are you sure that you want to go here?"

Of course I am certain. Would I have said so otherwise?

I hand the driver a bill.

"The rest is for you," I say generously.

"Thanks, thank you very much, Miss."

Since Danny will pay for all the expenses from now on, I can generously share his money.

The gate to the house is open. I am pulling my battered suitcase behind me and wonder what is awaiting me. I had not spoken with Danny since that momentous day and have no plan for the further flow of things.

With a clenched fist, I hammer against the enormous door. Then I see a small doorbell reflecting the sun. I hold the fingernail of my little finger next to it to estimate the size. A little hint on or next to the little button could bring it more attention and give the one ringing, in this case me, a certain advantage. Namely that of not being asked afterwards why you didn't use the doorbell.

The door is opened. A dour woman in a black dress and white apron stands opposite me and radiates a dry aura.

"Why don't you use the bell? I almost didn't hear your knocking."

Yes, that is exactly what I mean.

"Are you Miss Bergstroem?"

I nod.

"Please come in. Mr. Greyeyes is travelling. I will show you your room."

Obediently, I follow the prim lady and, lost in thought, look at her bottom. If they are all so friendly here, this really will be no bed of roses.

She leads me into a small, cozy room on the first floor with an adjoining bathroom. Apparently a guest room. This room is really tailor-made for me. Small and not too extravagant. A pretty desk in the corner with a view from the window. It could be useful for my work.

"Mr. Greyeyes' bedroom lies right next to yours."

"Thank you," I say and look at her inquisitively.

Is that somehow important? Naturally I would prefer that his bedroom be at the other end of the house, but why does she tell me that?

"By the way, my name is Mary. I am the housekeeper. If you have need anything, just call for me. There is someone in the house until 8pm. The morning shift begins at 9. Just for your information."

Nice, so now I am clear about the essentials. I don't need to know any more.

Mary leaves the room without another word.

So, fine, now I will settle in. With a jerk, I lift the suitcase on to the bed and open it. I search for my Laptop among the clothes and put it on the desk at the window with the wonderful view of the garden. Here I will certainly spend a good bit of time. I press myself against the powerful desk, to move it closer to the window.

So, that's enough. Now I have an eye on everything.

After I have packed away my clothing in the closet, I go on a spontaneous expedition through the house. There is certainly a lot to discover here. We'll see what I encounter.

Unfortunately, I don't get far because Mary intercepts me along the way.

"Oh, Miss Bergstroem, I looked all over the house for you. Mr. Greyeyes just called and inquired whether you have arrived. He says to tell you that, unfortunately, he won't be back until late and you don't need to wait on him."

I can't claim that that bothers me. There are really much worse things. For instance, having to live in this horrible house for three months.

"Thank you. I will definitely not wait for him."

When, after eight o'clock, all the personnel is finally off work, I go wandering out of curiosity. I move from room to room and, under the roof, discover a huge studio that could compete with the size of a gymnasium. Some guitars are hanging on the wall and the drums set up give the impression they had just been used. In the middle of the room, a black piano is sparkling as majestically as the Titanic on the open sea. Apparently it is a practice room, in which Danny will develop some of his pieces with his band.

Without a plan, I land in Danny's study during my rambling. Not that I had intended that – not at all. I don't snoop in the matters of other people – normally not – but my inner voice put me up to this inappropriate action. I can't help it. As I said, the voice …

Unintentionally, I sit down at his desk. But then, all by itself, my hand pulls a drawer open and rummages around in it. I only find a few boring little notes and nothing really juicy.

My hand opens a second drawer. I see a crinkled envelope. Immediately my nose moves deeper into the drawer. As if by magic, the letter lands in my fingers. Indecisively, I stare at it for a while until I decide on a short, harmless perusal of it. With a look around, I check whether the coast is clear before I take the note from the envelope. The paper is so worn that I'm afraid it could crumble in my fingers.

Concentrating, I read the lines. If I had succeeded with that on the day of the contract signing, then I wouldn't be sitting here now. The writer wrote with blue ink and quite illegibly. I have to read the last sentences of the letter several times. They depress me. They were signed by an Elizabeth. Only at the end do I understand. Elizabeth was his girlfriend in school. Shortly after the death of his parents, she broke up with him. How insensitive.

Quickly I fold the thin paper back together and put it back in the envelope. Carefully I put it back in its place and push the drawer to. I should be ashamed. Since when do I snoop in someone else's things?

Finally, I gain back the control over my unrestrained curiosity. Feeling guilty, I change over to the living room and try to keep my hands off all the objects in the house. Somewhat bored, I sit down on the large sofa and look at the fireplace. A few prepared logs are lying in it. Such a little fire could be quite cozy. On the mantel I discover a few matches. I decide to pour me a glass of wine in the kitchen and start a fire in the fireplace.

When the fireplace is crackling and snapping, I turn out all the lights in the house and sit down with my wine glass in the reflection of the fire on the sofa facing the fire.

I could doubtlessly enjoy such evenings. Very relaxing. In time, I get sleepy and snuggle up under a wool blanket that was lying over the armrest. The flames warm my face and eventually I go to sleep.

The clicking sound of a lighter causes me to awaken with a start. Danny is sitting in a chair opposite me and lights a cigar.

"Oh, I'm sorry. I didn't want to wake you. You seem to have settled in. I'm glad."

Don't draw any false conclusions!

"You don't need to think I could like it here. I'm only trying to make my non-voluntary stay in your walls as pleasant as possible."

Danny leans back smiling and draws on his cigar with pleasure.

"But you knew what you were letting yourself in for. You did read the contract," he asserts.

No, I did not. In any case, not on the day the contract was signed. Not consciously. If I had read these disastrous lines, I wouldn't be sitting in your living room now.

"And how did you imagine the further course of things?" I ask, somewhat irritated.

"I will send you a plan of my appointments for the following week. It is certainly in line with your wishes if we spend the next three days alone. We can start calmly and cautiously."

Certainly. That's completely to my liking. By no means could I imagine anything better than to spend my time continuously with him. How nice.

"On the weekend, you could accompany me to a party. If you like."

He finishes his last sentence with a derisive grin. Naturally, he knows that it doesn't matter at all whether I want to or not. For my signature on this sneaky contract obligates me to accompany him for all occasions.

"Yes, my pleasure. Thanks for the offer."
Just wait! I'll make sure that the laughter vanishes.

Irritated, I get up from the sofa.

"Good night!" I comment with an icy tone and go.

While I am lying in bed, I roll from one side to the other and reflect continuously on my hopeless situation. If I only knew how I could get out of this contract. The dull sound of steps in the hall is swallowed by the carpet. Oh, yes, Danny's bedroom lies directly next to mine. Hopefully he doesn't get the doors mixed up. Judging from the rumbling noises, he just entered his bed chamber. I press my ear to the cold wall, so as not to miss anything. But, a bit later, everything is quiet as a mouse. In case he is dead, I'll know tomorrow morning. I close my eyes and force myself to go to sleep. Yet I'm still listening into the stillness and simply find no rest. Only as the first birds start their morning chirping do I slip into sleep.

The next morning, we sit together silently at the breakfast table. While Danny, preoccupied, studies the newspaper, I stare at the bulging bread basket. If I only knew where my stomach is lingering. I would like to eat, but, after swallowing, food should not fall into empty space. It is clear to me that one should never begin a day without breakfast. But I simply can't get anything down. Not even a tiny crumb. Without having done anything, I get up and wander to the window. The weather is again unsurpassable. Plenty of sun for several days. I can think of some things to do with so much sunshine, if I weren't obligated to write this stupid book.

Danny looks at his watch.

"What would you think of a little walk in the park?

"You don't seriously think we could remain unrecognized there."

I don't believe I consider this to be a reasonable idea.

Danny smiles as he sips coffee from his cup.

"I mean the park around the house. Pack a pad and pencil. You should be making your first notes."

I wouldn't dream of it. Let that be my concern. Am I the author or are you?

Silently, Danny and I go through the little garden. At the end of the path, I see a pavilion, which Danny is resolutely approaching. Indifferent, I follow him. When we have reached it, I am amazed at the beautiful view of splendid flowers. Multi-colored rose bushes are growing around the greenhouse and are in full bloom. Without a word, we sit down at a little ornate garden table. The sweet smell of the roses lets me forget for a short moment. A warm ray of sun hits my face and, charmed by the captured moment, I close my eyes. I breathe in the summer air deeply and hold my breath for a moment. A hand touches my arm and brings me back from my paradise.

"I'm glad that you enjoy my company so much but, without a conversation, you won't get any material for your book."

Indignant, I pull my arm away and adjust my sitting position.

"Under these conditions, your company is anything but a pleasure for me. And I can get a good picture of you without a lot of chatter. You can just as easily write down important information or tape it. We don't have to spend every second together for that," I comment with a sting.

"Well, that's fine." Disgruntled, Danny bends over the table. "I had actually intended to go easy on you over the next three months. It hasn't escaped me that public appearances don't suit you. Under these conditions, however, I don't need to show any consideration for that. So prepare yourself for a very full calendar of appointments! I'll send you everything else by way of a typing pool."

Danny is irritated, so he gets up and goes. Insulted, I turn in another direction.

Wow, what a convincing performance! If you think you can bring me to your knees with your threat, you are deceiving yourself. I hold the reigns and, if you don't behave, I could consider incidental remarks in my book. The contract doesn't regulate how I have to formulate my view of you. A little gap in the contract to my benefit. Rubbing my hands, I lean back. He wants war and that's what he will get.

The Plunge into Cold Water

On Saturday morning, I find a note on the breakfast table.

Cocktail party this evening. Leave at 7 o'clock. Evening attire desired.

As you wish. Since my wardrobe has no evening gown – when do *I* need an evening gown? –, I will obtain one at your expense. That will indeed be a nice shopping spree.

After breakfast, I call a taxi and head for the most upscale stores in New York. Naturally, I ask the driver to wait on me while the meter runs uninterrupted. We'll see how high the taxi bill can get under these conditions. The sales ladies have their hands full with me, since I rampantly try on one dress after the other.

As it happens at the end of a long shopping expedition, I go back to my temporary home with a whole trunk full of bags. After all, I can't wear the same dress for every occasion. That wouldn't look right. So I used some foresight and got the complete wardrobe for the coming weeks in one fell swoop. That was fun indeed! I have to grin as I enter the house with my dozens of bags. Danny is awaiting me and pressing his arms on his hips.

"Where were you all this time? It would have been nice if you had left me a note that you intended to buy up the whole city."

Smirking, I walk by him.

"The whole city" will soon be deducted from your account.

In my room, I sort the content of the bags into my closet. After these three months, I could donate the clothes to the needy. What would I do with them at the North Pole?

At exactly seven o'clock, I am standing ready to march and waiting for Danny. Agitated, I play with the material of my dress. What is awaiting me at this party? Danny will leave me unattended, and I will have to see how I assert myself in this elitist, smug glamour world. They will soon recognize that a conversation with a goldfish is more exciting than my company.

Danny's hurried steps reveal that we are running late. Unaffected, I take note of his tardy appearance and wait on further instructions from him. He remains standing and his eyes move down, sizing me up. With the choice of my dress, I seem to have suited his taste. His gaze is really undressing me. Embarrassed, I dig around in my hand bag.

Danny's suggestive smile doesn't exactly help me in coping with my considerable nervousness, but rather leads to an increase in my pulse activity. Under these circumstances, a measurement device would run hot.

He seems a bit strange to me in his pin striped suit. Before, his outfit was more casual. But his informal and sporty manner of presenting himself in it seems convincing.

"Nice. You are on time. That pleases me. So shall we go?" he asks in his cool way.

In front of the door, the dark car with the shady driver is waiting for us. I get in the car before Danny and move as far to the back as possible. Danny sits opposite me in the large limousine and doesn't say a word to me during the ride. I can't say that this silence number is a problem for me, but admittedly it doesn't resolve the wearing tension between us.

We reach a mansion outside of the city. One senses the luxury that it diffuses from a distance. I somehow don't succeed in admiring it, although it embodies much style and elegance. Not to speak of the exaggerated size. The front is blocked with countless cars of the newly arrived guests. A domestic servant opens the door and leads us into the garden.

My breath comes to a standstill. The entire high society of the country is gathered there. People of the highest class are standing together and making small talk. Dozens of employees are swarming around them, to provide them with all the amenities.

A friendly older couple hurries over to us. Only now do I find out that Mr. and Mrs. Daniels are giving this party on the occasion of their fortieth anniversary. They are among the richest entrepreneurs in the area.

I congratulate them politely and am irritated that Danny has not said a single word. Perhaps I would have gotten a small gift – at Danny's expense, of course – or a suitable excuse would have occurred to me for not accompanying him. You don't celebrate anniversaries with unknown persons. And I am certainly a stranger to Mr. and Mrs. Daniels.

In a motherly way, Mrs. Daniels takes me by the hand and introduces me to more guests. I can't deny that I find her likeable. In spite of all reservations – I like her.

But I would be grateful to her if she would set me aside in a dark corner. Instead, she feeds me to the wolves, the whole group of party guests. I know she means well, but I feel so foolish. They are all staring at me avidly and forcing conversation on me. Unfortunately, my mouth is tied up like a package, and hardly more than three or four words make it out. It unsettles me that they all know who I am. A waiter holds a tray of drinks toward me.

"Take an aperitif, Miss Bergstroem," Mrs. Daniels says.

I consider whether I should follow her invitation, since I have only had alcohol twice in my life. And each time it had such a strange effect on me.

I'm not sure I would like to risk that again. Certainly not in this stilted society. No, I'd better keep my hands off this disastrous brew.

"Take one, Miss Bergstroem. Don't be so shy."

Mrs. Daniels gets a random glass from the tray and hands it to me. Bravely, I take it, as I look around for a pot of flowers suitable for an improper disposal of the spirits. She pushes me forward to the next guests, to whom she would definitely like to introduce me. I look around for Danny, but can't make him out among the many people. As expected, he doesn't give a damn about me.

Suddenly, Mrs. Daniels remains standing and waves excitedly into the crowd.

"Oh, there is my son!"

A good looking man in casual clothing is greeted eagerly by Mrs. Daniels.

"Miss Bergstroem. May I introduce my son Richard to you? He is our only boy and my pride and joy."

Oh, alas, she must have missed that her boy has matured into a grown man. Mr. Daniels junior looks at me with a charming smile and extends his hand to greet me.

"Miss Bergstroem. I'm extremely pleased to meet you. I've heard a bit about you."

I smile uneasily and look into his bright eyes.

"What have you heard about me?" I ask timidly.

Richard laughs, amused.

"Don't worry, Miss Bergstroem, my knowledge of you is limited to the content of your books. I pay little attention to the many reports in the media about your private life. Not even a third complies with the truth."

Yes, exactly!

Mrs. Daniels shakes my arm.

"Excuse me for a moment please. I think I have to greet a few new guests."

Immediately I sense a vacuum in my tummy. My stomach pulls together to the size of a pea. It becomes clear that I am being forced to converse with her son. I ponder intensely and search for a subject of conversation. But as soon as I am in such a predicament, there is an absolute void in my head. No chance to call up one single word from my memory. Baffled, I take a swallow from my glass, whose content has been bringing on a headache.

"Tell me, have you considered a project for a new book?"

Richard Daniels inquires with interest.

I choke on my drink and have to cough.

What should I reply? No would be a lie, but yes would be also.

Actually, I never considered this project. That would never have crossed my mind. Mr. Daniels pats me a few times on the back.

"Are you better now?" he asks thoughtfully.

"Oh yes. Thanks a lot. You know, I normally don't drink alcohol."

Richard Daniels nods sympathetically.

"Then it's probably best if we get you another drink."

He extends his arm gallantly. Hesitating, I take his arm and let him lead me to a quieter part of the garden. He beckons an employee over to us and asks for a glass of mineral water. Then he continues on his way with me until we reach an idyllic pond. For a moment, I enjoy the breather from the human setting. Yet the fact of having to experience peace with a stranger causes some uneasiness.

"I find that you are a very interesting woman, Miss Bergstroem."

So? Has he perhaps mixed me up with someone else?

"How did you end up with your unusual last name?"

"It's the name of my mother. She is Swedish. And, since my father had no official last name, they simply picked the name of my mother as the family name."

Surprised, Richard smiles.

"Why didn't your father have a last name? I don't understand that."

"In the past, many Inuit named themselves according to objects or landscapes. They simply didn't have a last name. My father comes from a very remote place on the east coast. At that time, many western customs simply hadn't gotten through. In the meantime, things are different."

"Interesting! I would like to learn more about you."

"Unfortunately, you'll have to put that off until another time, Richard!" I hear Danny say in the background.

Stunned, I look around and see his angry face, distorted with rage.

"Miss Bergstroem is my escort this evening. I'm really sorry to take her from you, but there is something we have to clarify with each other."

Rudely, Danny grabs me by the arm and pulls me away, without my having the chance to say good-bye to Richard Daniels.

He carries me off into a distant part of the garden, away from all of the activity. Submitting to my fate, I snap at him.

"What sort of a scene was that? What kind of liberties are you taking?"

"Do I need to remind you of your obligations? You have the job of staying close to me to get to know me better. Can you explain how that will work, if you would rather flirt with other guys?"

Indignant, I take my arm from him, which he was obstinately holding on to, to prevent a premature escape by me.

"I'm not flirting with any guys. Mr. Daniels and I were only conversing."

"Of course it was just a conversation. That's why it was away from the real function. Do you seriously believe that Richard Daniels only wanted a harmless conversation with you? How naive are you?"

His opinion of me truly seems to be contemptuous. Why is he getting so excited? It's my business with whom I talk. Anyway, it was charming the way Richard Daniels looked after me. You can't say that about Danny.

"You had suddenly disappeared and apparently didn't care about me. I can't help it if Mrs. Daniels introduces me to her son."

Danny's facial expression is like that of a gladiator in the arena. Apparently, it causes him great difficulty not to lose his composure.

"So that it is clear for the future: You remain at my side for all occasions! And only at *my* side! In case you should get on the wrong path again, I'll consider that as a breach of contract. Have I expressed myself clearly?"

Evidently, this contract is putting handcuffs on me. Or is it Danny who mercilessly wants to put me in chains?

"Am I your prisoner? I think I will be allowed to converse with other people?"

"I didn't know that it is important to you to converse with strangers. Up until now, I had the impression that conversation was unpleasant for you."

For once he is right. Nonetheless, it is my business with whom I talk.

Before I can reply to his last comment, Mrs. Daniels comes up to us.

"My dears. Why are you hiding at this lonesome place? Come on, the buffet line is open."

Danny puts his hand on my back and pushes me gently forward.

"Come on! We don't want to disappoint Mrs. Daniels."

I spend the rest of the evening silently at Danny's side. I observe him and acknowledge that he is a very good conversationalist. He knows how to entertain, put himself in the limelight or discreetly withdraw. His choice of words is always considered, and his tact makes him into a good listener. I could surely learn a lot from him in this regard. But it wouldn't be of any use. Being taciturn is something I inherited. My father talks as little as I do. No idea what my mother sees in him. She herself was equipped by nature with an all too active mouth, which only stops when she is sleeping. As if wound up, she talks to my father the whole livelong day. And yet he enjoys her presence. That must be true love.

Shortly after midnight, Danny is finally ready for our departure. I am very happy, since it is harder and harder to suppress my yawning.

Danny probably ran out of ideas on how to shield me from Richard's attentive looks. Whenever he directed his attention at me, Danny placed himself in his field of vision, to block his direct view of me. A highly devious way to behave. I don't believe it is written in our contract how often other men can look at me. Besides, he can hardly prevent this. Why should he even want to do that?

"Miss Bergstroem, it was really an extraordinary pleasure to have met you," Mrs. Daniels declares upon our departure. "I hope we will see each other more often."

"That would please me very much," I respond honestly.

Mrs. Daniels' warmth seems to be totally genuine – that's why I liked her right at the beginning.

On the drive back, I wearily sink back into the seat. Silently, Danny looks over from the opposite seat.

"I hope I didn't disappoint you the rest of the evening," I observe sarcastically.

His restrained reaction to my cynical remark surprises me. Only a short blink of his eyes allows me to see that he has noticed my words. But the expected backlash fails to materialize. His dimples dig pensively into his skin while he continuously looks at me. I would like to merge with his colony of brain cells and investigate them incognito. In spite of my curiosity, I don't urge Danny to converse but fall into my usual silence.

Finally we reach the house. After Danny and I have climbed out of the vehicle, we go silently together through the entrance. But as I want to creep to my room, exhausted, Danny surprisingly calls me back.

"I'd like to ask something else," he explains with a helpless gesture.

At this moment, his vibes are more those of a hurt child than of a combative adversary. So I swallow my resentment and look at him expectantly.

"Do you intend to see Richard Daniels again?"

This unexpected question makes me turn pale. Was he thinking about this the whole time in the car? He was concentrating on whether I could have come to like a man? I understand. He's got a new idea there. Actually, I had not thought for a second about this possibility.

"Why is that important to you?"

Impatiently, he is weaving around in place. His face muscles are beginning to twitch.

"Would you please simply answer my question!"

This interrogation is becoming annoying. That is my business and doesn't concern him in the least. I'm here to write about him and not to talk about me.

"It's getting too stressful for me now. I'm going to bed," I answer and, worn out, I continue on my way upstairs.

When I get to my room, I peel off my dress. The humid air this evening prompts me to take a cool shower. Maybe that will help me bring order to my chaotic feelings. His question agitates me, since it reveals more than he is aware of. Yet, under the circumstances, I wouldn't want to get involved with Danny. I feel betrayed by him because of the deceitful contract.

After the shower I wrap myself in a robe and step out of the bath into my room. I am shocked and startled when Danny is suddenly standing in the room. Without saying a word, he comes up to me. I try to dodge him and go back a few steps until the wall stops me.

"What do you want here?" I ask, confused.

His arm is leaning against the wall and the glowing look of his dark eyes reveals a sudden passion flaming up. Unrestrained, he pulls me toward him and forces his lips onto mine. I give up my resistance and hesitantly respond to his kiss. His arms embrace me more tightly and are cutting off the air.

If the circumstances were not as they are now, I would doubtlessly give in to everything. But the situation is that Danny has put chains on me and I am basically staying here against my will. In no case will I also allow that my pride be taken from me.

With all my strength, I press myself against Danny and push him away from me. Irritated, he looks at me.

"So it is this Richard Daniels!"

What? How can he think that?

Turning into ice, Danny lets go of me. There is bitterness reflected in his eyes which gives me goose pimples. The threatening stillness between us causes me to hold my breath. Danny examines me uncertainly. He seems to be searching for an answer. His glance wanders restlessly over my face. When I finally find my composure, he leaves the room. Dazed, I run my hands over my face and let myself slide down the wall, until the floor catches me. The minutes go by and I'm still sitting there. How can he dare to treat me so high handedly? He didn't even give me the chance to explain it to him. Why does he judge me prematurely each time? I never get a chance to justify myself.

If he acts this way with all other people, it would be astounding if he got to know one single person well.

I should try to talk with him tomorrow. His presumption that Richard Daniels could be the reason for my rejection is simply absurd. With my definite resolutions, I go to bed.

Deceptive Peace

I can hardly believe it when I see it out the window of my room the next morning. Danny is leaving the house with an angry stride. He goes to one of the parked cars and gets in. He revs up the motor and speeds off from the front with squeaking tires.

The search for a note or a little message somewhere in the house is in vain. Why should what he has dictated for me apply to him? In the future, then, I don't need to make any more reports on why I am leaving the house.

I trot to the phone and make a date with Lucy for this Sunday afternoon. We'll meet in front of a small café.

"Hey, Malina! Finally! Tell me, how are you doing? Are you getting along with him?" she inquires, as she gives me a hug.

Oh, Lucy! How nice to see a familiar face again. You don't know how very much I miss you. And my old life. If the time with Danny were only over with. I long for my parents and would like to know what my brother is up to. I feel isolated from the outside world.

We enter the café and sit at a little table at the window.

"Do I need to worry about you? You seem so different."

"No, no, don't worry. I just miss you so terribly. You and my old life. I long for the day when I'll be free again."

"So you're not getting along with each other? Tell me! How's it going?"

All at once it just pours out of me. Without taking a breath, I tell each little detail of all that has happened. When the latte is served, I still keep going. Lucy is stirring in her cup and listens attentively. All of my pent up heart ache pours out of my mouth like a waterfall.

"Imagine, today he took off without a word. No idea how it's going to proceed."

So, that was my last sentence. About an hour of the finest conversation material. Without having made notes before. Simply told off the top of my head. That just occurs to me.

Lucy shakes her head for relief and rubs her ears with both index fingers. That could be an indication of a sensory overload. Sorry. What is wrong with me?

"Malina, I don't recognize you anymore. You are talking without interruption. Danny's presence seems to have a good influence on you."

Pardon? Didn't she listen to me at all? Living together with him is like being an inferno! What is she saying? In my current situation, I expect more empathy from her. At least if she wants to claim to be a good friend.

I would like to have heard everything, but not that he has an influence on me. And certainly not a good one.

"You shouldn't give up, Malina. Maybe he is worth it."

Worth what? Okay, he has a lot of money. So, strictly speaking, he is worth a lot. But she didn't mean it like that, did she?

"I don't understand you," I comment.

"Write your book about him. You can do that. He is certainly not a bad person. Get to know him better first. At least try!"

Obviously. That would be the most reasonable. I hardly have a choice. The contract.

"You are right," I surrender.

She is always right. I hate that!

When we say good-bye, it is eight o'clock. I didn't notice how fast the time went by. And yet I don't have any desire to go back. Thus I decide to take a walk on this wonderful, balmy summer evening, so I can think about yesterday evening in peace. If he just hadn't walked off. I could have explained my feelings to him. I think. What is there to explain? You either have feelings or you don't. Do I have them? If this contract had not been so etched into my brain, then I would know the answer to this question.

A taxi drops me off in front of Danny's house about ten o'clock. The door squeaks as loudly as the hinges of an old trunk when I open it. From the foyer, I can see Danny in the living room and, determined, go up to him. The smoke of his cigar is floating like a white veil through the room. His eyes are resting on the fireplace and, although he has already noticed me, he doesn't deign to look at me.

"I would like to talk to you about something," I bravely start the sentence.

Without a word, he takes a drag from his cigar and sends the fumes in my direction, finally giving me his attention and looking at me. My hand is fluttering around in front of my face, to save me from the overpowering cloud of nicotine. Unfortunately only with moderate success. I almost wish that he would turn his glance away, since it is unpleasant to be so intensely examined by him. So what did I want to say to him?

To alleviate the tension, I sit down with him on the sofa. At the other end, however. For my own security, there are a woolen blanket and a few pillows between us. Should I put the hearth rug there as well?

"Surely it would be best if we could make peace for the time to come. And it would be useful for … our book (did I say *our book*?), if we were to sit down and talk about you a bit."

Did I want to talk about it with him this evening? Wasn't it a matter of something quite different? I can vaguely remember wanting to mention yesterday's incident. When it's necessary to talk, I seem to be blocked like a stopped up drain.

"I understand," Danny says casually.

Uncertain, I chew on my nails. Basically, I'm not a "nail chewer". But, at this moment, I am. It gives me more security. If I were to smoke, I would have no cause for this alternative activity.

Couldn't he say a little more? "Understand" sounds promising but doesn't really help me any further. Uncertain, I start again, a bit differently.

"You were right. If something is to become of this project, then we must work together. It's not much use to me, if I get all the information about you in writing. I have to be able to ask questions, to gain a better picture of you."

Thoughtfully, Danny looks at me and, for a while, he forgets to draw on his cigar.

"Where does the change of heart come from?" he asks skeptically.

Hm, that I can't explain so exactly. Maybe Lucy is responsible for it. Or, without knowing it, I was exposed to a brainwashing experiment of the CIA, in which people were randomly kidnapped on the street. Yes, that must have taken place during my walk.

"Without collaboration, it's not going to work. I understand that now. How would it be if we sit down together tomorrow?"

I suggest bravely. Danny shaking his head unsettles me. Did I again grasp at the wrong approach?

"It won't work tomorrow," he replies gruffly.

"Good, then maybe day after tomorrow?"

"Yes, maybe."

I'd only like to know what "yes, maybe" means. Possibly it doesn't depend on what I say, since Danny doesn't want any conversation with me. There's no mistaking it that I am disturbing him. Certainly there's nothing to be said against my going to my room now.

"Yes, maybe" I will write nothing at all about Danny, except that he is the most egocentric person of all time. For this, I only need one page of my book. For that would be sufficient to describe this person. That will become a best seller. Everyone will want to have it, because it can be read fast and effortlessly. You can read it here and there. A quickie. Maybe I could manage to formulate everything in a single sentence.

"You can let me know when your schedule allows it," I reply derisively and get up from the couch.

"Yes, sure. When ..."

Astonished, I look at him.

"If you're not interested in the book any more, you can say so. We would save some wasted time together," I comment, provoked.

"If you see it that way."

For crying out loud! This one-syllable behavior is real torture. Couldn't he finally say what he thinks and how he imagines our co-operation in the future?

"How is it going to proceed?" I ask, irritated.

You tell me.

I? Why me? Why can't he open his mouth?

"What do you want to hear?"

Danny laughs bitterly and leans forward to the table, to knock off the burned ash of his cigar in the ash tray.

"You know exactly what I mean," he answers angrily. "Don't act as if yesterday evening had been completely removed from your memory!"

Anyway. You won't believe it, but that actually happened to me during my walk. Against my will, I was robbed of my memory. Just like that. That's why I had completely forgotten before what I really wanted to say to you. But now, when you mention it, it occurs to me again.

"Listen," Danny begins, when I can think of nothing to say about yesterday's incident, "the best thing is to forget everything about yesterday and concentrate on the book. That would be the best thing."

So, I couldn't have expressed it better myself. That would suit me. Until the book is finished, I don't know what I want. First I have to get a clear head. And how will that work if my freedom is limited to a minimum?

With a short nod, I agree to Danny's proposal. He takes note of my silent answer, but is anything but cheery.

Despite our agreement, I don't see Danny on the following two days. It bothers me that I don't know where he's hanging around. I don't want this to concern me and I look for ways to distract myself. I try to free myself from undesirable thoughts with a meditation exercise and sit on my bed with my legs crossed. I close my eyes and put my hands on my knees (using the back of my hands). I concentrate my thoughts on a little ice floe, which is floating alone in the ocean. Slowly I begin to relax and float over the white ice shelf. The waves sway my ice floe on the water and everything seems to be in absolute harmony. But what is that? Shocked, I open my eyes wide again. What is Danny doing on my ice floe? Can't I find my peace anywhere? Again and again, these cursed thoughts circle around him. That is extremely inconvenient.

Suddenly I hear the front door close. With a quick glance at my watch, I check the time. It's already after eleven. Where was he prowling around so long? I hop out of bed and hurry down the stairs. Danny is just throwing his jacket over a chair and pouring a glass of cognac. Slowly I sneak up to him.

"Where were you so long?" I ask, somewhat rashly.

Surprised, Danny turns around.

"I didn't know that I had to account to you for anything."

"No, certainly not. That is not necessary," I reply timidly. "I just thought we would want to start with our work in the near future."

Looking down, I sit down on a chair and casually evaluate the tasteless color of the floor covering. On a scale of one to six, I would give it a four with a fat minus sign.

"We're going to do that, Malina. Tomorrow evening you'll again get the opportunity to accompany me to a casual gathering. There will be some press and television reporters present. But that doesn't matter to you anymore."

He empties the glass with one swallow and puts it back on the tray.

"It would be nice if you could show up around six in the evening in the foyer. Good night!"

Indifferently, he goes by me.

That hit home. Not a trace of consideration. Now he is driving everything home with all his might. Crushed, I fall back in the chair. And I, stupid girl, offer to make peace, so we can finish this book by mutual consent. You're not going to get me down. I'll show you! Don't think the little bit of press tomorrow could scare me.

Alcohol is no solution

Punctual, as I am used to being, I stand in the hall and wait. I am wearing the finest threads, which I acquired during my expensive stroll through the city. Certainly Danny is letting me wait on purpose. But I won't let him notice my resentment. I am more dissatisfied about the unending tension between us. This controversy with him bothers me. Feeling gloomy, I lean against the wall and inspect the chandelier on the ceiling. I wish we could start all over again.

When Danny arrives, I am deep in thought. I jerk as he suddenly speaks to me.

"So, fine, you are already here. Then we can get going."

Yes, I've been waiting a solid half hour for you. But that shouldn't bother you. That is probably part of your new harassment technique. I will bear it with composure.

Self-confident, I climb into the limousine. Danny follows a short time later and tells the shady driver to take off. During the drive, Danny is continuously on the phone. I don't listen and look absent mindedly out the window. But one conversation causes me to perk up my ears. It doesn't seem as formal as the others. More personal. His voice becomes noticeably softer. During the phone call, he almost immerses himself in the seats and bends more downward. The driving noises and his soft whispering prevent me from understanding the content of the conversation. Only bits of chatter reach me, of which I can't make a thing. I sense a budding jealousy. My stomach hurts, as if I had swallowed sharp rocks. If there were a man on the other end of the receiver, Danny would most probably be gay. But, since any rough estimation suggests he is not, he must be talking with a woman. A phone conversation between two men would never take place like that. I remember the rejection with which I hindered Danny's attempt to get closer. Why couldn't I allow it? It's no longer clear to me.

Shortly before we reach our destination, Danny quickly ends the phone call. I size him up as I look at him, trying to tell from his facial features what is happening with him.

"Why are you looking at me like that?" Danny inquires, bewildered.

I probably should have carried out my investigations less conspicuously. It is not my intention for him to feel I am spying on him.

Squinting, I look out the window and am shocked at the sight of the crowds who are gathered before the entrance of the festival hall.

"You certainly always wanted to go to a gala event," Danny sneers.

Naturally I would like that. A gala event? Good God! All the big names will be gathered here. Not to speak of the journalists and people from the tabloids. I'm lost. How can I get out of here? The car stops and our door is opened from outside. Now only one thing will help. Breathe in deeply three times and imagine you are on a large ice floe, surrounded by hundreds of small seals. Everywhere just seals. Nothing else. They won't do anything to you. They're completely harmless. Danny lets me go first. Naturally, I am the lady. As an exception, can't I be the gentleman? Just this one time? Please! Impatiently, Danny asks me a second time to get out of the car. Good. I can manage that. I can manage that. I can manage that. My right leg leaves the vehicle. A flurry of flashing cameras from all sides. Hey, that was only my leg! You airheads took a picture of my leg. I really do succeed in getting out of the car. Immediately I am surrounded by photographers. Do I have to pose now? Which part of my body is really my good side? Do I have one at all? Danny follows me and grabs my arm. Unnoticed by the cameras, he pushes me forward. Screeching hordes of people behind the fencing. Nothing but escaped lunatics. No, nothing but little seals. Don't look so carefully! Simply keep going!

Hardly have we reached the ballroom and a tray with champagne is handed to us. Quickly I reach for a glass. I desperately need something I can hold on to. All tensed up, I clutch on to it and look around.

In the distance, I observe how some attractively dressed women cheerfully pose for a camera man. Amused, they are giggling. You can notice their light heartedness. I could never be like that. Never ever would I willingly place myself before a camera.

We are going toward a cluster of people, and individual parts of it are already waving at us. Am I supposed to know them? No. But Danny. What great pleasure over seeing each other again. Exuberantly, the ladies greet my escort.

"Daaannyyy! Nice to see you here. How are you? Oh, you have your new girlfriend with you."

Ha!

They pay no more attention to me. Danny is being monopolized by them. If I am superfluous, I would like to know it now. I wouldn't mind just going.

"We hope you will sit at our table, daaarling. It will be a disgrace not to have you nearby."

What kind of smug broads are those? If Danny counts these types as his best friends, his distorted image of women doesn't surprise me. Now they are laughing so artificially. Where do you learn to do that? They take his arms, one the left and the other the right, and lead him to the tables.

So, now I'd like to know what role is being assigned to me. If some camera man has this ridiculous spectacle on film, then I am making myself into a laughing stock, if I am gullible enough to waddle behind this threesome. Clueless about what to do next, I look around. During my inspection, no cameras stand out that could take unwanted pictures of me. So, inconspicuously, I follow Danny and his newly acquired harem. When he has reached one of the big round tables with his crew of women, he actually turns around to check on me.

He hasn't forgotten me. Interesting! Should I wrestle for him like the other two ladies? Or is it sufficient if I discreetly sit at my place? Which one could be mine? I discover gold place cards and read my name in ornate writing. It's the place directly next to Danny. But one of the harem ladies blatantly trades her name tag for mine. Is there a reason to say something or should I just quietly accept it?

I decide on the latter choice. For Danny sees no cause to complain. Apparently he enjoys the flattery bestowed on him. Of course, I wouldn't have been able to offer this. I would first have to learn how to be clever and hypocritical. A worthless talent, in my view. I completely lack the aptitude for that. Such character traits are not necessary in Greenland. It makes no difference to a seal whether I like it or not, when I have my rifle pointed at it. I take my place and peek at the place card of my table mate. It is embarrassing that this name is totally unknown to me. I'm probably sitting next to Bill Gates and don't even know it.

When they have all taken their seats, I get to meet the person next to me. It is an older but very likeable gentleman with graying hair and a slight accent, which I cannot place. I really do not talk so much to him, but he talks to me.

He has many stories to tell from his eventful life. His tales interest me and distract me from this unbearable flirting between Danny and his harem ladies. If only the buffet would open, so that I could fill my empty, famished stomach. Naturally, it was nerves that robbed me of all appetite on this day. So I only succeeded in downing some emergency provisions. Unfortunately, these are long used up, and my metabolic engine is demanding replenishment.

While it is increasingly harder to follow the stories of my friendly table partner, I restlessly play with the stem of my champagne glass, which is still filled to the brim. When will there finally be manna?

A gracious woman with curly red hair enters the hall late. She is wearing a red evening gown. I have nothing against red hair, but the red gown just doesn't go with it. The two tones of red color scream of disharmony. Doesn't she hear that?

She waves to someone at our table. Interested, I look around. Whom could she mean? Danny looks up and gives her a sign. Danny?

She goes up to Danny, who receives her, very pleased. She kisses him on the cheek. Just like that. Why can she do that? One harem woman abandons the field. Little red riding hood sits down next to Danny. He immediately orders her something to drink. Somewhat too attentive, I find. They begin a casual conversation and look intensely into each other's eyes. My fingers are clutching the stem of the champagne glass so tightly that it threatens to break. Something is seething inside me. I am smoldering, and a lava flow is forming in my stomach, which might break out of me, beyond my control.

She giggles like a hen, who is pressing out an egg. What does Danny see in her? Granted, her aura is impressive. In spite of the mistake about the wardrobe. But she doesn't suit him. That is, as far as I can judge that.

Suddenly, the secretive phone conversation in the car occurs to me. That was *her*! Naturally! My rules about alcohol, which I imposed for my own security, fade and I take a big swallow from my champagne glass. The shock has to be somehow washed down. The moment the dangerous beverage reaches my stomach, I sense a tingling in my limbs. No wonder. The stuff is twice as vicious on an empty stomach. For me, always. I don't want to admit to myself why my feelings are going on a roller coaster ride. That would make me even more vulnerable. It's better to keep it under lock and key. Maybe I will wait it out.

No! Never! I can't face this another second. She's actually putting her arm around him. Again, a little champagne runs down my esophagus. The alcohol is hampering my reason and soaking up my capacity for logical thinking. Soon there will be nothing left of my brain. Everything just swimming around in alcohol.

Her arm pulls him closer to her, and their heads touch. Now that's the last straw! Seething with rage, I get up from my chair like a rocket and stomp over to them.

"Danny, can I talk to you for a moment?" I ask with a quivering voice, standing behind him.

Frowning, he turns around to me.

"Can't this wait?" he asks, irritated.

If you want a murder to take place, it certainly can wait.

"No!!"

Straining himself, he gets up and follows me through the hall. I discover a hidden door that leads into a side room. Exactly the right place, free of witnesses, to give Danny a piece of my mind.

"Why are you taking me away from the table? What is this about?" he asks, annoyed.

"Please tell me why you dragged me along here tonight? Maybe so I can provide an overview of how popular you are with the female sex? You wanted me to get to know the real Danny and to write about him, so the whole world understands who you really are. Is it actually the real Danny that this is about? Do you want to make yourself into a lady-killer? And what role did you intend for me, if I'm supposed to play a role at all?"

My eyes get watery. Dang! Hopefully no tears will roll. That would be most unpleasant. Just don't show any weakness.

"If I didn't know better, one could assume you are jealous," Danny comments, amused.

What a disgraceful assertion! Jealousy is almost foreign to me. What am I supposed to have been jealous about the last five years – completely without a boyfriend? So I don't know how something like that feels. A feeling unknown to me.

"Your assumption is completely absurd. If you are definitely of the opinion you have to present yourself to the world that way, then I won't keep you from it. You can do whatever you like."

Danny laughs and looks at me with indifference.

"You said it yourself. That's why it's unclear to me why you are so worked up."

I'm not getting worked up. Not at all.

"You have demanded from me that, during an event, I not move from your side. But now I have to share the place at your side with three other women. That is humiliating, and you can't require that of me!"

My eyes get watery, and so Danny seems blurry. Normally, I never cry. And it would be most appropriate not to do so now.

"No, you only have to share the place with Elizabeth. The others are only casual acquaintances. It would be nice if you would just do your job and keep discreetly in the background. And, if there are sources of disagreement between us, I would be grateful if we don't have to deal with them this evening."

These words take my breath away. The strong pressure in the stomach area is mysterious. Have I been stabbed?

Elisabeth?! I know the name! *This* Elisabeth from the letter? But didn't she drop him? What does she want from him? And what does he want from her?

I don't understand myself. Why are his words offending me to this extent? What sort of unfathomable pain is this in me? I lose myself in my feelings, seem to be drowning in this forceful distress, which is seizing my mind. My composure, my foresight – everything blown away. My body threatens to explode. The pent-up tears spill out.

"I hate you," I remark, but with a disciplined tone, and leave the room without a further word.

On my way to the powder room, I cover my tear-stained face from the curious looks of the press as much as possible.

"Miss Bergstroem! How nice to run in to you!"

Furtively, I look through my hands, which were positioned to cover my face. Mr. Richard Daniels runs directly to me so that my cover will be blown any moment.

"For heaven's sake. Are you not doing well?"

"Don't worry. I just got something in my eye. Please excuse me."

Quickly I head in the direction of the lady's room. That's all I need – that somebody is a witness to my weeping.

I close myself in the bathroom for about an hour and let my tears flow. Of course, with peaceful surroundings, I make every effort to concoct a battle plan for my campaign of retaliation. But nothing occurs to me. Nothing that would be appropriate. I have to try to endure this evening with some dignity. I consider everything else. Maybe I'll simply throw everything away. Even if I have to bleed from this contractual penalty for the rest of my life.

When I return to the hall, cheerful goings-on are evident. The buffet has been attacked and most guests are avidly enjoying desert. I am not the least bit hungry. Instead, I grab a new glass of champagne from a lonely tray.

You poor glasses. Did you get ditched like I did? I smile at the glasses and empty the glass in one swig.

"I must admit it is an extraordinary pleasure to see you again," I hear a familiar voice say behind my back.

When I turn around to reply to Mr. Richard Daniels' charming statement, I have some slight problems with orientation. My sense of balance is suffering rather considerable disturbances from the inappropriate intake of alcohol. The room extends into an infinite distance and, shortly thereafter, pulls back together.

"That looks like fun," I comment, delighted.

Mr. Daniels' face is subject to a similar physical change. This distorted sight amuses me.

"What did you do to your face, Mr. Daniels?"

Deliberately, he overlooks my intoxicated condition.

"Actually, I thought it was still the same one. Did something unusual strike you?" he asks, smiling.

"Well, if you ask me, Mr. Daniels, you should leave this room quickly. Just like this room, your face seems to defy all physical laws and is distorted. That really looks funny."

My giggling is out of control.

"Well, if that is the case, I would be pleased to accompany you, Miss Bergstroem."

Politely, he offers me his arm. I take it and let him lead me to the terrace where we are alone.

"I found it most regrettable that our last encounter had such a sudden end. Maybe we could take up where we were interrupted."

Actually, there is no reason not to. Only this top spinning in my head is a bit of a hindrance. I simply can't concentrate on anything.

"Fine. If you promise not to ask any complicated questions ... Hick!"

Oops!

Amused, he laughs.

"You are really enchanting. No, we don't have to talk if it is difficult for you. Maybe you would like to leave this place? If your present client has no objections this time."

In spite of my befuddled condition, I register the nature of his information, even though he portrays the cooperation between Danny and me with some misunderstanding. Or am I misunderstanding something?

"How am I to understand your remark?" I ask, smiling.

"I've heard that you are working together with Danny Greyeyes on a book."

"Yes, but how do you know that?"

His face is again subject to unnatural distortions, as are all of our surroundings. His nose is getting longer and longer, and it's coming toward me.

"Watch out, your nose is growing!"

Mr. Daniels composes himself, checking his nose, and, amused, starts to laugh. Apparently, he seems to join in on any fun. I like that. Under normal circumstances, I'm not in fact a real jokester, but I could work on myself a bit in this regard. The laugh lines around his bright eyes seem to be proof of his zest for life. That's exactly what I need now. For Danny's behavior this evening pulled the rug out from under me.

"What do you think of my proposal?" he inquires, as a diversion from the subject of the nose.

Was there a proposal?

"Pardon? ... Hick!"

"Miss Bergstroem, I don't want to offend you, but I think it would be in your own interest if I get you out of here. It hasn't escaped me that there seem to be differences between you and Mr. Greyeyes. It's certainly best if I drive you to my place," he suggests and wraps my hand around his arm.

"You certainly will not drive her anywhere!"

Danny appears suddenly and snatches my arm from Mr. Daniels.

"You have no scruples at all," he scolds Richard Daniels. "Kindly search for somebody else with whom you can play your games. I didn't know you have to make your victims submissive with alcohol, in order to get what you want."

Angrily, Danny tears me away. With a vigilant eye, he drags me through the halls past the cameras. The dark car with the shady driver is waiting directly in front of the entrance. Danny opens the back door and pushes me roughly into the vehicle. Unexpectedly, Richard Daniels is standing next to Danny and holding him by the arm.

"Danny, you really surprised me with your angry visit last Sunday, and I was inclined to give in to your request to stay out of Miss Bergstroem's way. But don't think I'm blind in both eyes. No details escape me. I wonder which of us is the real gentleman. Your banter with the women today is puzzling to me. And, contrary to your assumption, far be it from me to engage myself in a short adventure with Miss Bergstroem. Be certain that I will let no opportunity offered me pass by unused."

Without any reaction, Danny gets into the vehicle. The gazes of both men are threatening. Was this a declaration of war?

"Go, take off!" Danny instructs the driver gruffly.

My uncoordinated thoughts did not grasp everything that just happened, but one thing did stick. On that Sunday morning, when I saw Danny roar off, he clashed with Mr. Daniels. That's why he knew so exactly that the book was planned. If I see through everything correctly, then Danny must have forbidden any contact with me. It used to be my brother was responsible for this. But now I am grown up and can watch out for myself. Who does Danny think he is anyway?

The roof of the car bends toward the night sky. Quickly I look downward but the floor starts to distort itself in a peculiar way. The contours of my surroundings become blurred and whiz around me in a circle. I get dizzy and I lose the control over my head, which falls limply on Danny's shoulder.

"Hey, everything okay with you?" Danny asks, concerned.

"You know, it's not Mr. Daniels' fault. I only drank one single glass of champagne ... Hick! Only one. And the one tiny sip at the table. Maybe it was two ... Hick! Or three? I think I'm allergic to the stuff. That happens every time, even if I just sip on it ... Hick! That's why I don't drink anything, never again ... nothing. Never! Hick! But

154

today I experienced such a strange thing. A fellow went with me to a gala event … Hick! And then he gave me a kick in the backside. In the middle of my face … Hick! I mean in the backside. It doesn't matter where. But that hit home. And you know why? Hick! Because he hit rather exactly. Right in the middle. Into the center. There where it hurts the most … Hick! But probably I deserved it. Hhmmh … that was my just punishment. I wanted to talk with him the next morning, right after that. That is, after the afterwards. You know. Honest … Hick! But then he suddenly drove off and I had no more opportunity. In the evening, I suddenly remembered nothing any more. As if everything were blown away. Did you ever get brainwashed? Hick! That must be what happened to me. Couldn't remember anything. The whole time I had considered intensely what I wanted to say to him. Doesn't matter. Now it's not important … Hick! Not important any more." My eyes get heavy and I let them close peacefully.

When I wake up in the same night, I am lying in my own bed. My dress is hanging neatly folded over the back of the chair. What? When did I take it off? I didn't! Pale from the shock, I push the button of the lamp on my night stand and cautiously peek under my bedspread with one eye. Relieved, I let down the corner of the spread. I still have my underwear on.

It's shortly after midnight and I haven't been lying here for even an hour. Did Danny go back to the gala event, after he dumped me off here? I'm sure he did that. After all, he can't simply have left his new, old acquisition in red behind. Elisabeth. I wish I were her. She's probably as close to him at the moment as I would like to be. But I had my chance. And now it is lost. Because I am too inexperienced with my feelings.

A soft rumbling in the next room causes me to sit up and take notice. Is he in his bedroom? Why didn't he go back to the gala event? What is with Elisabeth? Curious, I crawl out of my bed and sneak out of my room, so as to gingerly steal my way to Danny's door. I listen carefully. Nothing. But did I just hear something? In breathless suspense, I dare to open the door slightly. Dim light comes through the slot, and so I open the door a bit wider and stretch my head through. The bedroom is empty, but something is moving in the adjoining bath. To get a clearer view into the bath, I have to go two steps forward and enter the room. The floor boards crunch under my feet and reveal my presence. Before I can flee from the room unrecognized, Danny steps out of the bath into the bedroom.

Without saying a word, he just stands there, holding a towel in his right hand and looking at me. Suddenly I am aware that I neglected to put something over me and took up my investigations in underwear.

"I … I … I wanted …" *Crap, what did I want?* "… I only wanted …"

Now I see that Danny is also standing in the room with only his underwear on. I direct my attention to his unclothed body parts, almost all except the one, and I am shocked to find that the sight of each individual part provides great pleasure. Is it possible that a person can come from such a perfect mould?

I would like to have seen the construction manual for this body. His tight boxer shorts show off his hot backside; only that is not the body part on which my eyes are resting now. Good, I know myself that a glance at his rear would be more harmless than the spot which is currently attracting my eyes like magic. If the packed up part is just as scrumptious, I would like to know now what is evading me because of my dumb misbehavior. If I could just have a short glimpse. Into the unfathomable depths of his boxer shorts.

"Are you doing better now?" he asks, breaking through the silence.

"Yes, I think so. At least until now."

But now I have to struggle against my elevated pulse, so I can't say exactly whether my regained positive condition will last.

"I'm glad," he comments and throws his towel on the bed. At the same moment, he heads in my direction. But he steps close by me to shut the door behind me. Surprised, I watch him.

Why is he closing it? I'm here. Didn't he want to first remove me from his room before he simply closes the door? Then he left out a serious step. How could he forget that?

Surprised, I point at the door with my finger.

"You forgot me. I mean, shouldn't I go out first, before you …?"

Danny is still standing next to the door and smiling.

Maybe I could take a short look at the covered centerpiece now.

Slowly I go up to Danny, who is standing there as if firmly rooted. He seems baffled by my unexpected action. Did he seriously believe I would wait until he takes the initiative? That takes much too long.

As I stand in front of him, I finally discover the fire in his eyes that once burned for me. My gaze wanders from his face down to his upper body. A few hairs are curling on his chest and inviting me to touch them. Only with effort do I keep myself under control. My eyes follow the hairy street on the stomach, which arises under the belly button and flows down the valley to the boxer shorts. I hold my breath when I again come to the bulges hidden behind material. This time, the amount of bulge could have multiplied. My urge for discovery prompts me to let my fingers wander along his waistband. But before I acquire any dumb ideas, Danny reaches for this hand.

"What are you doing with me?" he whispers. "You're driving me crazy. I want you more than anything else. But, if you are just playing with me, then I need to know it now."

But that is more than I would have dared to hope. Then I haven't lost him to this Elisabeth?

"I have never played with your feelings. Only my uncertainty has stood between us. Haven't you noticed that? This contract. It didn't allow me to think clearly. When I signed it, I was out to lunch. I felt under pressure and thought you were not being honest. I'm sorry. I …"

Danny's hand is stroking my face.

"Forget this contract!"

Without a further word, he pulls me to him and kisses me passionately. Little surges traverse my whole body and I wouldn't dream of resisting his tenderness. I am enjoying the moment much too much. Finally, I can let my hands wander over his back and stop at his backside, so as to inspect the curves with my fingers. The last known rear I held in my hands is now married to my former best friend, and this is much too long ago. So I'm taking great care with this inspection. But these measures do not distract me from my real interest. The zone still unknown to me. While Danny pulls me toward him, even more intoxicated, and our tongues eagerly circle around each other, my hand is seeking its way forward. Enraptured, I feel the warm swelling. Unfortunately, almost at the same time, Danny prevents me from any further excursions.

"Hey, you can't wait for it," he murmurs in my ear and lifts me onto the bed.

Viewed soberly ... only sex?

The sun shines in to Danny's room as we wake up together on the following morning. I am lying in his arms and dreamily reviewing the past night. If it were up to me, this night would never have ended. It is not that I have no sexual experience. That is, my private life in my first and only relationship was quite acceptable. However, not to be underestimated is the five year period of abstinence. After this eternity, one might say of a man that he is starved. But I never got tired of it at all. In recent years, however, it never struck me that something was missing. Not until now, when I have it again. So, sex. Viewed soberly, it sounds a little bit unromantic. But, seen factually, it was a question of nothing else here. Additionally, I have to emphasize that Danny is an extraordinary lover. Without a doubt, there would have been no night of love with another man. For me, the one thing belongs to the other. It has finally become clear that Danny is more important to me than I wanted to admit the whole time. Yesterday evening finally opened my eyes. I'm in love with him. My wall, which I enclosed around me the last few years, has fallen. I'm again daring to allow feelings. That I may still experience that! I painted my future as being without men. Would have been all right. Until yesterday. But now I can no longer imagine a life completely without "XY chromosome". Maybe Danny would be willing to be my

"XY chromosome" for the rest of my life? But what's with Elisabeth? Does she perhaps still play a role in his life? Am I too late? Was I just an interim high for him? It would have been smarter to have carried out a thorough investigation of this not insignificant matter ahead of time. But who works with his reason when hormones are going crazy? Presumably, it's happened to me. Something I never wanted to allow. To be an open box of chocolates. Danny got it on with me. I enjoyed it. And that was it. Now I can go.

His arms are wrapped gently around me.

"Good morning," he breathes into my ear and gnaws on my ear lobe.

Yes, keep doing that. I should savor the last hours together with him as much as possible, before it is all over.

Worried, I look at him.

"Is something wrong?" he asks, concerned.

No, what's supposed to be wrong with me? I just have the most exciting night of my life behind me and realize that it will never be repeated. That is depressing.

"Danny, I don't know if I have the right to ask you this, but is there something between you and this Elisabeth?" I ask, hesitating.

"Oh, that's what this is all about," he remarks, composed.

He moves away a bit, which lets me conclude that my assumption is falling on fertile ground.

"I've known Elisabeth since we were in school. We are just good friends. Nothing further."

Aha! She really is it. The Elisabeth from the letter. And so I know immediately that they never can just be good friends, because there was more between them, which he plainly doesn't think worth mentioning now. That makes me wonder.

Danny comes closer and kisses me on the nose.

"I can see by the tip of your nose that you don't believe me."

Oh can you?

"Honestly, I am not certain," I admit.

"She is not important, believe me. You are the only thing that counts now, okay?"

Okay, and how long do I count? Until Elisabeth is important again?

His hands wander down my body and caress my skin. That could lead to a revival of my passionate energy, which is resting for the moment. I should warn him. But, before I can say something, he is lying over me and kissing my neck with desire. If that's how it is, it's impossible for me to succeed in resisting. I can think about Elisabeth again after this. Now there is something more important. My hormones are calling again.

I have lost my feeling for time during the last hours. And I can't determine exactly which day it is. Thus I have resigned myself to simply knowing what is really decisive. That I felt more happiness in the last hours than in the last five years. That scares me. What if my happiness bursts like a soap bubble? Could I find my way back into my old life? A door has opened into a new world. I am enjoying a sample from it and sense there is no more turning back for me. I could never carry out my old life again. My self-imposed isolation and beloved loneliness would no longer be sufficient. I want more!

Danny and I sit in the kitchen and fill our stomachs with everything the refrigerator has to offer. Now I am trying out the delicious home-made plumb jam of Mrs. Mary, when I drip some on to Danny's white T-shirt that I am wearing.

"Oh, the sumptuous plum jam just spilled on your T-shirt." Amused, I giggle as Danny avidly tries to lick the jam from the T-shirt.

"Don't be so wasteful with Mary's plum jam. It is extremely valuable."

He pulls the shirt over my head.

"Let me see. Have you hidden any of the jam here?"

I laugh with wantonness as Danny searches my stomach for the rest of the plum jam with his tongue.

Suddenly he pauses and looks at me pensively.

"What is it?" I ask, waiting for him to answer.

Come on, keep going! I could hide a little plum jam in my navel.

"You are really amazing," he remarks all of a sudden. "Since I met you, I've been continuously questioning my previous life." This unexpected confession gets my attention. "Everything you do seems so honest. You give hope to the people you write about. By making public their history and their lives, you make known their grievances. Your work is valuable and important. I admire them. I admire you."

His hand strokes my cheek.

"You really mean me?" I inquire skeptically.

It's possible that his clear-sightedness has been blurred by last night. Intellect driven by hormones can lead to an unintentional error. Who could admire me? And for what? I am really nothing special. More of a simple average type. If anything.

"It is really incredible how such a pretty woman, who has experienced and accomplished so much as you, can be lacking in self-esteem."

It is slowly becoming unpleasant for me that he has, in my opinion, an inaccurate image of me. I am only me. What is so commendable about that?

"You are overestimating some things. Believe me," I reply critically.

Laughing, Danny shoves the rest of the bread with jam in his mouth. I observe him chewing. Could it be that this is really his unwavering opinion of me? How can I make it clear to him that he is wrong? Can't conceive what will happen when he realizes one day that I am only myself and nothing further.

"Malina, you should know that you have impressed me from the very beginning. I'm seriously considering changing some things in my life. But first I have to settle some different things. I should have done it long ago. I have put it off far too long. But now, when we are so close, I am absolutely certain."

What is he talking about?

"I can't completely follow you."

"This evening, I will do the job properly and finish with something which hasn't meant anything more to me anyway. Heaven only knows why I haven't done it sooner."

"What do you mean?"

"Later. As soon as I have resolved everything, you'll find out. Now it would likely agitate you too much. I wouldn't want to upset you."

But you are! I want to know now on the spot what this is about! Come on! Out with it!

"Please, talk with me *now*," I plead with him. "My father always says that it brings bad luck if you put something off that you could take care of immediately. Maybe you won't get another chance for it. Please share your thoughts with me."

Firmly Danny shakes his head.

"I think it would bring us bad luck if I hadn't ended it beforehand."

What does he want to end? What does he mean, damn it?!

But Danny can't be moved.

"Please accept my decision and simply trust me."

With this, he ends the conversation and leaves the kitchen.

Well fine! If he had just given me a little tip. Then I would not be in the dark like this. Where does he want to go today? And how could that upset me? I simply must know. So I will insist that he inform me about his plans. Determined, I stomp behind Danny to his room. He's standing dressed in the room and smells like men's cologne. Immediately a qualm spreads out in my stomach. And, since I am a woman, this gut feeling almost always has something to it. It has never appeared without a reason.

With an imploring look, I hope for his understanding.

"Don't worry! I'll be back in a few hours and then we can talk about everything."

I try one last time.

"Is it about the contract? What do you have to resolve that I may know nothing about?"

"My God, you twist everything around. It's not about this contract. Forget it once and for all! It's not important any more. It never was."

This statement stuns me.

"The contract isn't important? But what is all this for?"

Danny comes up to me and takes me in his arms.

"Do you seriously believe it was only a matter of you writing a book about me?"

Actually I thought that, yes.

"It wasn't that?"

"Let's talk about it later. I have to go now."

No! Don't! Stop it! A new puzzle again. Give me at least a letter! How many boxes does the answer have? One letter. Only one. Please!

With a short wave, Danny says good-bye and disappears through the door. Feeling blue, I sink onto the bed. There's nothing for me to do but to wait until he is back.

The hours go by at a snail's pace. Incessantly, I am busy checking the time. I could repeat the seconds in strict time without making use of a second hand. I have almost mutated into a clock when the phone rings about eleven o'clock. Excited, I reach for the receiver and am amazed when I don't hear the voice at the other end I expected. A young woman's voice asks for me.

"Is this Malina Bergstroem?"

"Yes, speaking."

Who is that? How does she know my name?

"My name is Elisabeth Palmer."

At this name, I stiffen into a pillar and have trouble holding the receiver to my ear with my cramped fingers. The red Elisabeth! What of all things does she want from me?

"Listen, Miss Bergstroem! What I am going to tell you now will certainly not please you. I would just like to save you any possible grief. You shouldn't hope for too much as far as Danny is concerned. He and I have been a couple since our school days, you know. Now and again he goes astray, but he always comes back to me in the end. This little liaison between you two is nothing further than a nice adventure for Danny. Don't wait for him this evening. He's with me, and that's where he will stay. Do you understand, Miss Bergstroem? You should forget him as quickly as possible."

What is she saying? That can't be! I don't understand it!

"I think that he can tell me that himself, Miss Palmer. So please let me speak with him personally."

"I'm sorry to have to tell you this, but his interest in speaking with you is limited to an extreme minimum. Good night, Miss Bergstroem!"

A crackle on the line reveals that she has ended the conversation.

What a bad joke. The question is where it comes from. Is Danny really playing games? Is that conceivable? I refuse to believe that. Certainly he will be back right away.

But where did she get that about Danny and me anyway? I didn't know myself until yesterday evening. He must have been at her house. Nobody else could have informed her about it, since, be-sides Danny and me, there isn't a soul who knows about it. What if what she maintains is right? If he is still with her and just used me? Is that what I was anyway? An open box of chocolates? How can a person feign something like this? With this talent, he should have become an actor and not a singer.

Stunned by this painful call, I sit down on the sofa and stare into the lifeless fireplace. My head is empty, and my rigid glance fixates on the same place without interruption. I would likely still be aiming at it apathetically until the next morning, if my fatigue didn't overpower me. Before I have drilled through the spot targeted, my eyes close.

I awaken at seven in the morning. My head lay on my shoulder the whole night, so that an over-stretched nerve in my neck begins to burn when I lift my head. Au! I prop up my heavy head with my hands and swing it a few times from left to right, to loosen the stinging nerve in the neck.

But all the effort is in vain.

As soon as I move my head, the pain goes down my whole neck. As if it took joy in bringing me additional suffering.

An extensive patrol through the house brings me certainty: Danny really did stay away the whole night. So it is right after all. What this Elis-abeth said on the phone is true. Why in the world did I let myself be blinded like this? How could it not strike me that absolutely nothing of what

Danny said yesterday is true? Never in my life have I been deceived in this way. I don't understand all of this. My rusty insight into human beings desperately needs an overhaul. Then such a disaster would surely not have taken place. Now it is again becoming clear that I have spent too much time with Arctic animals instead of with my fellow human beings. I simply have more experience with animals. Seals, for instance, are incredibly sociable and always stick together when it matters. They never disappoint each other. At the present, I would prefer their company. Instead, I had to get involved in Danny's dishonorable games.

So I'm going to again take up my considerations of settling at the North Pole in the future. Some especially lonely spots would come to mind. There where I can be sure of never having to encounter anyone else in this world. Absolutely not one single person.

My eyes accumulate fluid. Since I encountered Danny, that happens more often than I would like. The last time my tears gushed out was when Phil revealed that he would rather be together with my best friend of that time than with me. Certainly he made the right decision for him. Whether it was right for me, I still don't know today. In any case, it led to my roaming through life like an ice block for the next few years. I allowed no more feelings and, since then, there has been no more spontaneous outpouring of tears. Now I am gaining practice again that I don't want.

Frustrated, I proceed to my room and pack my things. I leave the clothes I charged to Danny's expense account hanging in the wardrobe. A last walk through the house awakens painful memories. I hope you are proud of your work, Danny Greyeyes. You can rightfully claim that you are a fantastic actor. If I ever get to it, I will voice some recommendations with the most renowned directors for you. Now, since I am so very prominent, it shouldn't be difficult to form appropriate connections with film and television.

I am really grateful to you for everything. You turned my whole life upside down. Nothing is as it was. And probably it never will be again. My peace of mind is down the drain. I am standing in the limelight and am naked. Completely exposed. There is nothing more the public doesn't know about me. They know more than I do. Every day I read new headlines about myself in the newspaper. My face will soon be known in every corner of the city. I never wanted to live like this. But Danny has made me the laughing stock of the people. First he pulled me into the spotlight, and now he is letting me fall like a hot potato.

In the midst of this chaos, I must attempt to bring order to my life again. I succeeded at that once, but the conditions were different. I was alone. Nobody knew me. I started practically at zero. But now I had to work back slowly from the hundred to the zero again. Quasi a regression. In the case that that were possible, do I want it at all? There is one think I want for sure: my peace.

With my suitcase in tow, I leave the house around nine o'clock. At that moment, Mary comes toward me.

"But, Miss Bergstroem, where are you going? Are you moving out? Has Mr. Greyeyes been informed about this?"

"It will certainly not interest Mr. Greyeyes where I live from now on. In the meantime, other things have become more important to him."

Bitterly, I pull my suitcase by Mary. I sense her questioning glance in my aching neck.

Don't act as if you didn't know what a heartbreaker your boss is! You dense, ignorant battleaxe!

Press Commotion

The taxi driver is already waiting for me at the gate. When he sees me approaching, the driver instantly gets out of his vehicle to free me from my suitcase. Finally somebody who thinks.

"Aren't you this writer? What was your name?"

"Malina Bergstroem," I answer, to give him a helping hand.

"Oh yes. The little lady who is in a relationship with Danny Greyeyes."

How nice that they all know my face but nobody knows my name. I am only the "little lady", who once was together with Danny Greyeyes. This little one would now like to go home. She would like to take a hot, relaxing bath and hole up in her apartment for the next few weeks.

When the taxi turns into my street, a huge shock overcomes me. The entrance to my house is blocked with television teams, reporters, and curious onlookers. Lucy is standing among them and trying to assert herself against the superior strength of the media. What is she doing there? Is she giving an interview?

"Should I really stop in front of this house, Miss Bergstroem?"

Oh well, if I only knew myself. Unfortunately, the house has no back entrance. But I want to go home. Into my bathtub. So I have to get through.

"Yes, please."

He does as I ask him. I wave to Lucy as I get out of the taxi. All eyes are directed at me. I take my suitcase from the driver and pull it on the way to the front door, while the journalists gather around me and hold their microphones in my face.

"Miss Bergstroem, what do you say to the marriage rumors about you and Mr. Greyeyes?"

Marriage? What sort of fantasies are they devising in their rumor mill? Crazy! All of them are crazy!

"Malina?! What are you doing here?" Lucy calls to me.

Tediously, I try to shed the bothersome vultures with their cameras and microphones. But they stick to me like Super Glue. Along with my inner conflict, there is enormous irritation about this crowd around me. Can't they finally leave me in peace? You want to have fodder? Then you will get it now.

"Listen," I say to the journalists all of a sudden, "there is no more reason for you to besiege my dwelling. The only reason why I got into the public eye at all was that you falsely assumed that I was together with Danny Greyeyes. Please take note once and for all that there is absolutely nothing to this. There is nothing between this Danny Greyeyes and me, so you need to get the picture!"

One of the reporters breaks away from the others and fights his way through the crowd up to me. When he is standing right next to me, he grasps my arm and drags me through the entrance of the house.

"It doesn't matter what you say, Miss Bergstroem. The whole world is convinced of a romance between you two. You have simply been seen together too often. I'd like to give you just one piece of advice: Accept your popularity. Learn to deal with the press and the public. I know that it doesn't suit you. Anyone who has read your first book understands what an enormous adjustment the big city of New York must have been for a shy, gentle person like you. But this here is something different. Approach people. Open up. They want more of you now. The ball got rolling and it can't be stopped. If you don't act soon, then they will tear you apart, Miss Bergstroem. Adjust to your new circumstances. It's for the best."

With these words, he withdraws and disappears in the crowd; but first he casually slips me his calling card. Distraught, I am standing alone at the house entrance. Lucy pushes her way up to me.

"Who was that? What did he want from you? Why are you here?"

"Which of your questions should I answer first?" I ask helplessly.

Lucy links arms with me and pulls me forward. As we enter our apartment, everything suddenly seems so removed. I wasn't gone that long at all. Three or four weeks at the most.

Apathetically, I trudge into the bath and turn on the faucet of the bathtub, while Lucy is brewing coffee for us in the kitchen.

What did the words of this reporter mean? Can it really be that there is no other solution for me? Do I have to surrender to the public? I know another possibility. Drowning in the bathtub. Only you can't breathe right. Maybe I could simply plop the hairdryer in the water by mistake. The stupid thing about it is that the plug is too far away, and the length of the cable would thwart my suicide attempt. I could drink Lucy's nail polish remover or …

"Oh, here you are."

Lucy comes into the bathroom and disturbs me during my self-destructive considerations. Nothing will ever become of this. How am I supposed to come up with the right method, the shortest one with the least pain? I need peace for this. Everything must be thought out exactly. It won't do for me to make a false move at the end and have people make fun because I don't understand how to properly take my last breath.

I strip off my clothes and climb into the warm water. Lucy hands me the coffee cup and sits down on the edge of the tub.

"Oh, Lucy. I am probably responsible for everything. I am really too naive. Danny was right. How dumb of me to assume I could honestly mean something to him. Somebody wrapped me around his little finger faster than I supposed. If it only didn't hurt so much. Now I'm really in a mess. Little Cinderella must turn into a butterfly and would rather stay where she was. Can you tell me what's next? I don't want this life I've been maneuvered into. It makes me afraid."

"What should I suggest, Malina? You have no more influence on how things will go. You have no other choice than to wait for further developments and accept them."

"Something like that is what the reporter advised before. He said I should surrender to the public and not run away. That would be the best thing for me."

Until lately, I knew what was best for me. But now I am absolutely clueless.

"Probably he is right," Lucy observes.

It's easy for Lucy to say. Being center of attention doesn't bother her. I, on the other hand, have been a shadow of myself all my life. How am I supposed to manage with a new life from one day to the next? This is just too fast for me. What was that with Lucy's nail polish remover?

"By the way, your brother came by yesterday. He asked about you."

Yes, that's how Namid is. Always on the scene when I am in a tight spot.

"What did you tell him?" I inquire.

"Well, I told him everything."

Fine, Lucy. Reveal all the secrets that I tell you! Does a reliable friend do something like that?

"What do you mean by everything?"

"Where is the problem? After all, he is your brother and worries about you. But never fear, Malina, we didn't just talk about you."

Yes, it really doesn't matter what she tells him. He only needs to open the newspaper and then he'll know what's going on.

"So, what else did you two talk about?"

Suddenly Lucy has such a mischievous facial expression. Did I miss something?

"Maybe less talking. More … well …" She clears her throat. "I hope it doesn't matter to you?"

"Speak plainly! What should not matter to me? Is something cooking between you two?"

"Yes."

Rolling my eyes, I submerge myself for a short time and consider under water what strange constellations have developed. Danny and I: that is strange. Lucy and Namid: that is even stranger.

Lucy and I have lived together almost five years, and never was there the least indication of a budding passion between the two. Until now, Namid has never been serious about a woman. It is possible that he could disappoint Lucy. I don't want that! Isn't it enough that I was disappointed? Now my only pillar of moral support does not need to also experience heartache. Slowly my head again floats to the surface. Through a flower of foam, I look at Lucy, smiling.

"You and Namid? I never dreamed that could be possible. But you know that he never lasted more than a few days with a woman?"

Worried, Lucy looks at the floor.

"Yes. That's why, as much as possible, I stayed out of his way."

"Did you have an eye on him for a while? Why didn't you ever say anything?"

I wipe the lather from my face.

"Because I didn't want him to find out anything."

"But I wouldn't have told him anything," I say indignantly.

"Maybe I would have wanted you to tell him sometime. Since I didn't know that you could get burned with your brother, it was the best. If I hadn't been alone with him yesterday, my tactic of suppression would have functioned for a while. Unfortunately, your brother left nothing untried to make it with me. I simply got weak."

This klutz! I'll have a thing or two to tell him. How dare he lay my best friend? How can I unload my trouble with her, if she is carrying around some of her own?

"And how is it going to proceed with you two?" I ask awkwardly. "Is it going to continue? Or was it just a one-time phenomenon?"

"Don't know."

The tone of voice perplexes me. Namid will be sorry if he has broken her heart- then he'll get a nasty surprise from me. He couldn't have picked a better time for it. Now of all times, when I need Lucy desperately. Oh Namid! May you be cursed!

Two weeks go by and nothing happens that could correct my picture of Danny. No phone call, no word of apology. Nothing. And Namid doesn't get in touch with Lucy. I tried several times to reach him by phone. No idea where he is. It's as if he disappeared from the scene. I would so have liked to ask him a few questions. For instance, why he had to break Lucy's heart, of all people? Since then, she is totally different. She hardly talks or eats. Comes home late and disappears in her room without a word. If I just knew how I could help her?

Of course I have enough to battle with my own distress. That is really the first time that I condemn Namid for his lifestyle. Let him knock up his brainless disco chicks, but not Lucy. What was he thinking? Goes into hiding and doesn't even contact her. How does he think Lucy feels? Can it really be that it doesn't matter to him?

To take my mind off things, I sit down at the computer. I don't know what is prompting me, but something in me is driving me to write the book about Danny. Perhaps I'll try in this way to come to terms with my bitterness about him. Or, unconsciously, I'm seeking a suitable means of revenge. Although neither my introductory words nor the following text put him in a bad light. At least not yet. But maybe I could change my mind.

The impressions I have gained of him in a few weeks, along with the written material about his past life that he gave me, convey a rather precise image of him. That will doubtlessly be enough to compose an undistorted autobiography and show an objective evaluation of the true Danny Greyeyes. I'll reserve the right to mention his overt wear and tear on women.

That depends on my future wrath about all men of this world. If Namid doesn't contact Lucy any more, I won't rule out the possibility that this will have a spontaneous and critical influence on Danny's biography. I could project all my bias about men in general – of course, unconsciously – onto Danny and inadvertently weave this into my book.

This way, I could kill two birds with one stone. I would have gotten Phil, Danny and Namid in one fell swoop.

However, I doubt whether that would make me happier. So I should not overestimate the deceptive power, which lies in my hands with this book. In the end, nobody has anything to gain if I don't maintain my objectivity with my work.

The telephone distracts me from my ripened thoughts. At least the caller has given me the time to bring my thinking to a conclusion. Nothing is more unsatisfying than to seek solutions for a problem and constantly be kept from finding them. For instance, I haven't come a step further in the question of the nail polish remover.

"Hello?" I say into the receiver.

"Miss Bergstroem, is that you speaking?" a familiar voice inquires.

It just doesn't occur to me why it seems familiar. It is clear that I have heard it. But where? It's rattling in my brain.

"Yes, it's me. With whom am I speaking?"

"This is Richard Daniels."

I've been struck by lightning. Richard Daniels is calling *me*. Me. What can he want from me?

"I hope I'm not calling at an inconvenient time."

"But not at all."

No. You couldn't have picked a better time. Right now I have time. All the time in the world. I am just finished with thinking, so to speak. Now it suits me perfectly. Talk! What does a Richard Daniels want from me? The aspiring entrepreneur's son of all times. Rich. Good looking. Charming. Educated and greatly sought after. I am commonplace. He dialed my little meaningless telephone number. And he dialed it himself. I assume. No female voice interjected in between connected me. He was just on the line. As I was. Now I am supposed to say something. For instance, that I am very pleased about his call. But I can't get anything out. Good grief, am I suddenly agitated! My pulse has my blood shooting through my veins and is bringing an unusual glow to my ears.

"Miss Bergstroem, I assume that my call is rather a surprise for you."

Well, yes, I can't exactly claim that I had counted on it.

"Perhaps a bit," I have to admit.

"I won't keep it a secret that certain passing remarks in the media have prompted me to take up contact with you."

What remarks is he talking about? And why "passing"?

"Without a doubt, I am aware that certain statements in the press are to be enjoyed with caution and their credibility is questionable. Thus I am allowing myself to contact you directly."

"I don't understand what you are getting at. Is there something I should know?" I inquire anxiously.

"Well, I'm not sure about that. Or do you think it is absolutely necessary for you to know that Mr. Greyeyes was seen together with Elisabeth Palmer?"

Ouch! Now it seems to be official that they are a couple. So what this Elisabeth told me on the phone was really correct. New proof for the accuracy of my assumptions. I was betrayed and used by Danny. He is infinitely hateful! Maybe I should make a satire out of his biography. I and the readers would get a lot of pleasure out of that.

"It's not at all necessary, Mr. Daniels, to inform me. It doesn't interest me in the least what Mr. Greyeyes does in his free time."

He should go jump in a lake.

"I hoped that you would say that."

So?

"Miss Bergstroem, I make no secret of the fact that I like you very much and was fascinated by you from the moment of our first encounter. I'm sure you've noticed that."

Well, yes, not I, but it was apparent to Danny. I'm as blind as a bat when it comes to such things.

"Honestly speaking …"

Should I say no now? That would be impolite and a "no" never comes out of my mouth.

"… maybe a little bit."

"Make my day and go out with me. Accompany me on my next business dinner. I desperately need a charming companion."

"Oh, Mr. Daniels, please don't take it personally, but I don't think I would be the right choice for that. You most certainly need an articulate companion, which I am by no means. It's possible I will scare off your business partners with my terrible lack of sociability. Whenever conversation would be helpful, I am silent as a grave. If you want to steer toward bankruptcy, you just need to regularly insist that I accompany you to your business meal."

Amused, Mr. Daniels laughs. But he doesn't give up, as if he had not recognized the seriousness of the situation.

"You are fun, Miss Bergstroem. Believe me, it has long been known that your belief in yourself is lacking in certain situations. In my opinion, this is absolutely unfounded. However, I hardly think there is a single person who objects to this. Your readers are crazy about you and admire your genuineness. In no case should you change this."

No? I may remain as I am? But the reporter was of a quite different opinion. So what is right?

"Don't you also find that I should surrender to the public interest and come out of my shell? Do you really think it's beneficial to shut myself off to everything?" I ask Richard Daniels inquisitively.

After all, he must know. His experienced dealings with public life are admirable. Again, exhilarated laughter at the other end.

"No, for heaven's sake! Where did you get that idea? For whom would it be advantageous if you surrendered to the media? For the media themselves, but not for you. You'll see what comes out of that. You'll become the play thing of the journalists. Simply try to shield your private life as much as possible. With your little tragic flaw, any other behavior would be sheer suicide."

I understand. So the reporter wanted to entice me. He certainly wanted to do that. Why else did he slip me his calling card? Maybe he was hoping for an exclusive interview with me. Why do I allow myself to be deceived so readily or be taken for an idiot? I have to listen to my inner voice and not always let myself be upset by other people.

Richard Daniels' words provide me with some self confidence. In the last week, a lot has fallen by the wayside. I need to find myself again, but it's just not working at the moment. It's possible that a date with Mr. Daniels will distract me and take my mind off things. It is good to hear that he doesn't have the slightest reservations about a possible meeting of his business partners and me. So I could lean back informally and let him talk. Simply sit there and observe him during his negotiations.

"You're right, Mr. Daniels. I could never transform myself into a new person overnight and do not want to stand in the limelight. I'm just not made for that. If it doesn't matter to you that I am not talented at speaking and your business that evening is ordained to go under, I would like to accompany you."

"I will take the risk with pleasure," he replies with amusement. "May I pick you up tomorrow around seven o'clock?"

"Fine. I'll look forward to it," I answer honestly.

You are seldom alone at a casual dinner

Punctually at seven o'clock, the doorbell rings. Cheerfully I open the door and am surprised that Mr. Daniels himself is not standing on the threshold. A chauffeur in blue takes off his cap and greets me cordially.

"Good evening, Miss Bergstroem. An urgent appointment came up for Mr. Daniels and he is sorry that he couldn't come himself. If it's acceptable to you, I'll drive you to the appointed meeting place. Mr. Daniels will be waiting for you there."

I didn't know that I had agreed on a meeting place with him. Where might that be? No, I'm not going to inquire. I'm not going to expose myself. There's no reason not to let myself be surprised. I just nod and follow the assigned driver silently to his vehicle. A big dark blue limousine. A VW bug would have worked as well. I truly feel lost in this massive car. Main thing is I find my way from inside back outside. The vehicle is almost as big as an urban bus. During the ride, I sit right up next to the door and look patiently out the window.

This time I'm not nervous. I'm almost looking forward to this evening, although I'm aware that Mr. Daniels' business partners are unknown. And, normally, this certainty robs me of all my courage. Since I know that Mr. Daniels is not disturbed by my reserve and a conversation between his business partners and me is not important, I can appear there relaxed. Just now we stop at a traffic light and I notice a news stand that is just closing. The headline of a newspaper literally jumps into my field of vision.

"Elisabeth Palmer, the Winner!"

The light turns to green and we continue our ride.

Then I call out to the driver: "Stop! Please stop immediately! Pull over!"

Bewildered, the blue man puts on his blinker and stops one intersection later.

"Wait a moment, please. I'll be right back."

I climb out of the vehicle and hurry back to the news stand. At the last minute, I catch the owner before his well-deserved closing time and get the one last paper from him.

On the way back to the car, I unfold the newspaper and cringe a second time at the sight of the headline. Only now do I notice that a small picture of me is printed next to Elisabeth Palmer's over-sized photo. There you are, in proportion to my picture, the interest in me is becoming less. Apparently this Elisabeth seems to enjoy the lime-light.

Let her do that. She can have everything: glamour, fame and Danny. I want nothing of it. When I'm sitting in the blue limousine again, I read through the article. But the very first quotations from Elisabeth Palmer pierce my heart.

"She (this means me) *is not at all his type. Much too quiet and plain. We all make mistakes."*

I was no mistake! You red toad! Maybe Danny got it on with me and abused my feelings. But I was no mistake. That nasty bitch!

Mortified, I crumple up the paper and throw it indignantly on the seat. I have to immunize myself against these shameful attacks on my person. If only they would bounce off of me. Since Danny has torn down my wall, I am vulnerable like a tree without bark. If I don't repair it fast, I will soon be a field of rubble. Everyone is digging in my wound. Now even this Elisabeth. Why is she doing that? After all, she has him back again. Am I really as plain as she maintains? And what is wrong with that? Would it have turned out differently with Danny if I had the temperament of a Spanish flamenco dancer? It has never bothered me so much as now that my liveliness doesn't go beyond the level of valium. Never did I have the feeling that I am a mistake. Now I do.

We arrive at a small, not too extravagant Chinese restaurant. Is the business dinner taking place here? Wow! I hadn't expected that it was being held in an average setting. That's very pleasant for me. The blue driver parks the dark blue limousine. I see Mr. Daniels, who heads directly for us. He opens the car door and helps me get out.

"Miss Bergstroem, I am inconsolable that I couldn't personally accompany you here, but …"

"… but business has priority. Of course I understand that, Mr. Daniels," I say to complete his sentence.

Happily, I smile at him and let him lead me over the parking lot. This evening, I am thinking about nothing at all and simply enjoying everything there is to enjoy.

"I thank you for your obvious understanding. My work completely monopolizes me. Unfortunately, too little time remains for private matters. I hope you really don't mind."

"But not at all, Mr. Daniels. I'm looking forward to it. If you really guarantee that I don't have to utter a word, then virtually nothing can happen to me."

Amused, he laughs and presumptuously puts his arm around my shoulder.

"Don't worry. I'm with you. So, really, nothing can happen to you."

Light heartedly, I smile at him and consider what reasons there could be for my being so uninhibited around him.

"Then I'm relieved," I comment before we enter the restaurant. The waiter leads us to our table. Mr. Daniels' business partners haven't arrived yet, so we have some time for a private conversation. So I use the opportunity to ask Mr. Daniels a question.

"Tell me, Mr. Daniels, why does a renowned man like you go to eat with a little, insignificant person like me? I mean what's behind your phone call from yesterday?"

Thoughtfully, he moves his hand over his chin and looks for the right words.

"How do you mean that?"

Well great! The question was clearly a mistake from my non-existent bag of tricks.

"I'm sorry, Mr. Daniels. I didn't want to be indiscreet. Of course my question was somewhat inappropriate. Normally, I am simply quiet and then I can't say anything wrong."

What must he think of me now? To ask such an ill-considered question right at the beginning is really unprofessional. So that it becomes clear that I have no idea whatsoever how to act appropriately on a date. I am really a total idiot!

"But of course not," he comments forgivingly. "Your question wasn't inappropriate at all. Perhaps a little direct. But not inappropriate. Not at all."

No? It wasn't so wrong at all? Not so much as I thought? Pooh!

Relieved, I fall back into my seat.

"I thought it is obvious that I like you very much, Miss Bergstroem. When I encountered you the first time in my parents' house, I immediately succumbed to your aura. Only I couldn't explain this peculiar relationship between you and Danny Greyeyes. But, on the next day, my questions were cleared up. I received an unexpected visit from Danny, who wanted to prevent me from having contact with you. I admit that I found his performance strange, but I respected his wish. It was not my intention to destroy your relationship. But, when I encountered you at this gala event, I suspected larger differences between you. The last headlines in the paper confirmed my expectations. Allow me the observation that I can't completely understand Danny's new choice. However, his decision is not without its advantages to me. I hope you don't misunderstand this remark. For me he is, stated succinctly, a dummy."

Yes, you really could characterize Danny that way. In my opinion, this description is too harmless. But accurate. Don't think that anguish will cause me to wall myself in an igloo, Danny Greyeyes! As you will soon see, I can amuse myself exceptionally well without you.

Only it is not completely clear to me why Danny went to Richard Daniels on this Sunday morning. Why did he demand of Richard that he stop courting me, when he was only looking for an amorous adventure with me in the first place? Under these circumstances, it shouldn't have mattered to him if another man was interested in me. Or am I overlooking something?

My glance moves to the entrance, as Richard Daniels' business partners blow in, a bit late. I start to cramp up and my feet are swinging restlessly in step. Mr. Daniels grabs for my hand.

"You don't need to worry. Nobody expects that you participate in a conversation. Simply enjoy the food. Is that all right?"

Relieved, I nod my head.

Mr. Daniels has such a comforting manner. I almost find it too bad that my participation in the conversation is not expected. Maybe I could make an observation now and again, just something in passing. We'll see.

The two gentlemen greet me as if they are delighted.

"Miss Bergstroem, I could hardly believe it when Mr. Daniels informed us that you would be here this evening. I am really most pleased. Please do me the favor and sign this book for my son," the heftier of the two asks and hands me one of my works. They both know me? One of their sons knows me? Danny really did a good job of it. It's disturbing that so many people know me. I thought I was here incognito.

"Very happy to," I answer and write a short greeting in the book.

If more people now recognize my face, I'm going to run screaming into my cave or disappear in the underground. Give me back my anonymity. Immediately!

The rest of the evening we talk about my books. No trace of any business subjects. Are those the right people who sat down at our table? Exhausted from talking, I excuse myself and slip off secretly outside the door, to be alone for a moment. Although my stomach was filled with healthy delicacies, I feel like a stuffed vacuum cleaner bag. But there could be other reasons for the malaise. After all, I am not used to so much conversation. No wonder that I feel as if some-body had pulled the plug to my energy supply.

I breathe in deeply and try to keep the oxygen in me before I exhale. So, that's a good feeling. A dark vehicle stops directly before the entrance to the restaurant. Looks exactly like …!

The car door is opened from inside, and I rec-ognize Danny and Miss Red alias Palmer sitting in the vehicle. A flash penetrates my heart and leads to an increase of my uneasiness, which I knew how to control up until now. I quickly hold on to the railing of the steps I am standing on. Breathe calmly. In and out. In and out.

After Danny has gotten out (before Miss Red), he sees me standing on the steps in front of the restaurant. My wounded heart does a somersault from agitation, while my second hand grabs for the railing. Just don't break down now. I have to get through this with dignity. Probably he'll give me a condescending look and go by without a word. That's how heartbreakers treat their victims when they have reached their goal. Isn't that right? Since I never before succumbed to a wom-anizer, I naturally don't know exactly, but the as-sumption makes sense.

Miss Red hasn't seen me yet and is busy with the folds of her dress. But Danny, confused, looks over to me and actually comes up to me. That can't be. What am I going to do now? My fingers are tensed up and clutch the railing, so that my knuckles shine through, as if they were gnawed off. My indisposition is transformed into dizziness.

When he stands directly in front of me, his eyes look at me inquisitively. Why is he looking at me this way?

"Malina!" he suddenly speaks my name.

I would like to say something, but the spinning top requires my full concentration. Miss Red has the folds in her skirt under control and calls for her companion: "Dannyyyy! Dannyyy … please come on!"

Danny' dimples say a lot. Unfortunately, I can't understand them. I simply don't understand his stunned reaction. This is not at all typical for a womanizer. I assume.

Little flashing stars are mixed up in my field of vision. Oh God oh God oh God! If I could only beam myself away!

Possessive as she is, Elisabeth pulls Danny by the arm to the entrance of the restaurant. He stops looking toward me only when he has disappeared through the door of the restaurant.

So now I can quietly faint. Exhausted, I sink to the floor. But my consciousness remains clear. The shooting stars before my inner eye slowly disappear and I succeed in taking a deep breath. Not much time remains for my revitalization, as Richard Daniels unexpectedly comes out of the doorway.

"For God's sake! What happened?"

Concerned, he bends over me and moves with his hand over my face.

"Oh, I got a little dizzy. The stale air in the rooms must have been the reason. It's all right now."

Awkwardly, I grope with my hands for the railing, so as to pull myself back into the vertical position.

"No, wait," Mr. Daniels says as he intervenes. "I'll help you."

Faster than I would like, I'm standing on my legs again.

"I'm going to take you home on the spot."

Before I can respond with anything, he leads me to his car and gives the driver waiting there appropriate instructions.

"Please drive up there and wait for me in front of the restaurant! I just need to clarify everything with the gentlemen."

"Oh please, don't break off your important business conversation on my account. I can't allow that."

"Believe me, there is nothing at the moment that I view as more important than your well being. Don't worry about my business. That can wait."

With these words, he slams the car door and again proceeds to the restaurant.

Some minutes later, we are sitting together at the back of the car and are being driven to my apartment. The strange glance of Richard Daniels unsettles me. His noticeable taciturn manner also puzzles me. What is suddenly with him? Did I do something wrong?

When we stop in front of my house, Mr. Daniels gets out before me and extends his hand.

"It is certainly best if I accompany you to your apartment door. I want to be sure that you get in unharmed."

Silently, I let him lead me up the steps and consider whether I should invite him to my place for coffee. Lucy is certainly out and about, and so we would be undisturbed. The question is whether my aim is to be undisturbed with him. On the other hand, there is no reason to continue to live in abstinence. I should finally begin to change my life. An amorous adventure or an affair would be a good beginning. I just wonder whether I place increased value on it. In this regard, I have absolutely nothing in common with Namid. But I could try it anyway.

"Would you like to come in for a coffee, Mr. Daniels?" I ask him, as we are standing in front of my apartment door.

An astonished look appears on his face. Did I again dare too much?

"I'd love to. But you are doing better now?"

Sure! For a while. Did I forget to mention that? I recovered from *this indisposition amazingly fast.*

"But yes! Much better. So?"

With a clear nod toward the entrance, I invite him to step into the apartment. He follows my invitation with no resistance. I only hope I don't regret my action again. Mr. Daniels might be an interesting man, but am I far enough along to indulge in new adventures? Only because my one "I" has seen that it is reasonable to forget Danny does not mean that the other "I" really can. The consequence would be that my "total I" would actively resist the re-allocation of my feelings to a new contender, and my coffee invitation would have been made for nothing.

But I should leave nothing untried. Viewed selfishly, it is a matter of restoring my ailing mental state. Mr. Daniels is just fine with me.

While I am brewing the coffee in the kitchen, Richard Daniels stands at the kitchen table and observes me. A few times I turn to him and smile.

"I must say you surprise me," he says, ending our silence with this observation.

Yes, I surprise myself. And I don't have a birthday for three months.

"What do you mean?" I follow up.

"Your unexpected indisposition, then the surprising recovery, and next the nice invitation into your apartment. I wouldn't have expected so much fearlessness."

"Pardon?"

What is he talking about? I don't completely understand the meaning of his words. Or I understand them much too well? He thinks I had planned it all like that. But I didn't do that at all. How does he get that idea?

"Do you think I had contrived all that? You're judging that completely wrong. I really was not doing well in front of the restaurant. If I had suspected that you would interpret it that way, I would never have invited you. You have to believe me!"

Heavens, what an awkward situation! Apparently it was a mistake to invite him in. I desperately need tutoring on how to deal with men. Lucy, I declare this to be your most essential assignment. From now on, this thing has absolute priority! His hands are on my shoulders and turn me around to him. He holds me with a firm grip.

"Malina, I must know if Danny means something to you."

These rapid changes make me confused. I was just thinking that I need a few suggestions on the rules and customs of a rendezvous. But now it appears as if Richard Daniels needs some instructions. Does one approach a lady so quickly and attack her with such a blunt question?

"Please excuse my aggression, but it has hardly escaped me that your indisposition must be connected with Danny Greyeyes. I saw him enter the restaurant. If I am conjuring false hopes, then please tell me."

Okay! Wait a minute! First things first. He certainly does know the behavior for a rendezvous. Only anxiety is clearly plaguing him as to whether

I still feel something for Danny or not. So he urges me into a confession I can never make, since I myself don't know exactly how much Danny still means to me.

Silent, I look at him and try to put an answer together. But nothing occurs to me. Does that prevent us from having coffee together?

"I'm sorry, Richard, but I can't answer that question exactly. I admit that it hurts me when I see him together with this Elisabeth Palmer. But I also know that it is sensible to forget him. I don't know how much importance I should attach to my feelings. If this answer is not sufficient, perhaps it would be better for you if you go."

"Oh, but it is. This answer is completely sufficient," he replies, surprisingly.

Oh my! I insulted him.

"Don't worry. I understand your words quite well. That's why it's really better if I go now."

This reasoning doesn't completely make sense to me. On the one hand, yes, and on the other hand, no. Why is it?

"But why? I mean stay … the coffee …" I reply, irritated.

"We'll make up for it. Maybe some time at my place, if you like."

He grabs for the jacket he had shed and goes to the door. Distressed, I follow him and stare at him with an imploring look.

"Please don't go! We could get to know each other better. I mean … talk."

"I know what you mean. But I think you need a little time. I would like to give it to you. If I were to stay here, I couldn't guarantee anything."

With a kiss on my forehead, he says good-bye and goes.

The Red Surprise

Luckily, it didn't take as long as I expected until Richard Daniels contacted me again. Actually, he hardly let five days go by. Didn't he want to allow me some time for sorting out my feelings? I found right off that this would not be necessary. Time doesn't help me with this at all. But what should I have done? Richard was firmly convinced of his action. Until yesterday. Then he called me in the morning. To my delight. A break in our contact was anything but right for me. After all, I would like to continue my investigations in matters of love. I must find out whether anything is lying dormant in me.

His parents have invited me to dinner for this evening, and I am flitting excitedly through the apartment. I regret that I left behind all the newly purchased clothes in Danny's closet. They could have been useful to me now. At least one of them. Luckily I made a find in Lucy's closet. A red dress. Whether it's chance that I got my hands on this color, of all things?

Around seven o'clock, I leave the apartment and drive my car to the villa of Mr. and Mrs. Daniels senior. I am looking forward to seeing Mrs. Daniels again. She possesses such a well-meaning openness that appeals to me.

As I reach the Daniels' estate, I can make out Richard's blue limousine from afar. So he is already there. But it's a mystery to me who owns the little red vehicle next to it. I thought I would be the only guest. In front of the door, I am greeted by Mrs. Daniels, who is beaming with joy. In a motherly way, she presses me to her breast.

"Miss Bergstroem, how nice that you could come! We are so pleased!"

Mr. Daniels arrives and clasps my hand.

Politely, I greet them both and hand the lady of the house my oversized bouquet, which I ordered a day earlier in the florist of Lucy's parents. It is the fault of Mrs. Atkinson herself, Lucy's mother, that the bouquet is as big as a medium sized shrub. When I told her who the flowers were for, she talked me into the extra large version, and I understood the necessity of this right off. Little people, little bouquets. Big people, big bouquets. This way, she made it unmistakably clear that anything else was out of the question.

Perhaps I shouldn't have listened to her, since Mrs. Daniels almost completely disappears behind the bouquet, while Mr. Daniels takes possession of it and carries it off. Mrs. Daniels links arms with me and leads me into the house.

"I must warn you, dear Miss Bergstroem. We have an unexpected visitor today. You will certainly be surprised."

Hopefully, she's not talking about Danny. I was just trying to clear my head for Richard. If I were to meet Danny, I would have to begin from the outset with my efforts to bury him from my thoughts. That is ineffective and pointless.

"Who are you talking about?"

But, when I have finished formulating my question, it answers itself and raises ten times as many new questions. This evening, the color red seems to dominate. Elisabeth Palmer is standing next to Richard and conversing with him. I am dreaming this. What does she want here? How do they know each other anyway? And why is she talking to Richard of all things? Is she out to get all the men I encounter?

Quickly, I calculate my chances in a battle with her. She is a half a head taller than I, and her whole stature seems substantially more compact. With all probability, I am physically far inferior. So a wrestling match can be declared in advance as lost. Since my strengths are also not exactly of a verbal nature, it would be smarter to keep quiet.

I also lack the necessary time to develop an effective battle plan, with which I could catapult her not only out of this house, but as far as possible out of my field of vision. So I ask myself the decisive question: She or I? We both are one too many. That much is clear. I'm the scheduled guest and she's the unexpected visitor. So who has to give way? I don't need even a second to answer this question.

All the same, I consider voluntarily clearing out. Solely for the sake of peace. But, as I am planning to tell Mrs. Daniels about my suddenly stricken aunt, who is supposed to be my excuse for the planned premature departure, Richard looks over at his mother and me.

"Malina! There you are, finally. May I introduce you to my cousin Elisabeth? I believe you two are already acquainted."

"You can say that again," Elisabeth says to me with her nasty manner.

Whaaat? She is his cousin? Her of all people? Why? I mean what was Mother Nature thinking about? There are so many cousins in the world. In huge quantities. So, the selection would have been just about limitless. But no, creation declared her to be his cousin! I find that outrageous!

Now I also understand why Danny knows the Daniels. I had wondered why they invited him to their anniversary party and why Richard and Danny always called each other by first name. Since Danny and Elisabeth were or are a couple, he will have met her family. And, as I have to experience, the Daniels belong to it. Wonderful thing! Now I would just need to merge with Richard, and we could arrange nice tea parties or foursomes with Danny and Elisabeth.

So, fine. She is Richard's cousin. Gradually, I'm recovering from my little shock. But what does she want here? What does she want this evening of all things? She could appear any other evening or morning or afternoon or day. Did she have to pick this one of all others? Is she waging war against me?

In spite of my reservations about her, I extend my hand as a greeting. Frowning, she looks in another direction.

"Good evening, Miss Palmer," I say to her, unflinching.

"Elisabeth, child, where are your manners?" Mrs. Daniels is amazed.

Reluctantly, she greets me with a short nod and proceeds to the door shortly afterward.

"I was planning to go anyway. Oh, Miss Bergstroem, it pleases me that you found a replacement so fast for Danny. Good luck with Richard! He is certainly a better match. Good choice. You apparently know what counts. Not bad for an ordinary girl from the sticks."

With these words, she opens the door and disappears. Full of dismay, Mrs. Daniels holds her hands in front of her mouth. Richard just blankly shakes his head and puts an arm around me.

"I must apologize for Elisabeth. She just …"

"But not at all!" I interrupt him. "You don't need to apologize for something for which you are not responsible. It's not a problem for me what she says."

Yes it is. It is very hard on me. But I would never admit it. My father always says that one only needs to have some patience. All pain inflicted one day finds its way back to the perpetrator. I have patience. Lots of it.

My tension, which is gradually easing since Elisabeth has left the stage, is causing further turbulence in my circulation. The result is that well-known dizzy feeling. My goodness, that is slowly becoming a habit. If that is going to occur regularly from now on, then an emergency packet would be advantageous. Maybe a paper bag or a body guard, into whose arms I could fall. My hand fumbles around and searches for something to hold on to. The color is drained from my face. Where is my blood? Everything is stuck in my feet. I am being pulled downward, as I black out.

When I come to again, I'm lying on a sofa. Richard is kneeling next to it, while his parents are standing behind him and looking down from above.

"She's opening her eyes," Mrs. Daniels notes, relieved.

"Child, what are you doing? We were sick with worry about you. How are you?"

Don't worry, that happens to me often. The dizziness is quasi an extra organ of mine.

"You were definitely unconscious for a few minutes," Richard interjects, worried. "At our last encounter, you weren't doing so well. You desperately need to have this checked by a physician."

By no means! My circulation was never especially reliable. It is like the weather. Unpredictable. That's nothing.

"Yes, I'll do that," I answer.

The rest of the evening we sit in the dining room and listen to family stories, which Richard's father knows how to tell. Naturally, they mainly involve Richard's childhood adventures. Since he is their only child, their parental love is concentrated exclusively on him. Richard seems to have no problem with it. While his father divulges one anecdote after the other from Richard's childhood, Richard just smiles contently. I enjoy this harmonious togetherness and keep peeking over to him. His eyes also scrutinize me continuously.

At a late hour, Mr. and Mrs. Daniels withdraw to give Richard and me the opportunity for a personal conversation.

Meanwhile, we are sitting with flickering candle light in the living room and chat exuberantly with one another. I feel comfortable in Richard's presence and I enjoy being with him. Is that good enough? Is that sufficient for a whole lifetime? Perhaps my mother would have been a good romantic adviser in this matter. When she decided on a life of solitude with my father, it was true love. Otherwise, one cannot accept such a fundamental transformation of his life. She exchanged her secure life in Sweden for the drab wilderness, to spend the rest of her life there at the side of my father.

Could I live on a lonely island with Richard? Would he be enough for me? Probably I am asking the wrong question. Since I am completely satisfied with just myself, a life with only one single person, regardless of where and with whom, would be rich in variety for me. Preferably, I would find out that his physical proximity sends out electrical impulses. Naturally, the best thing would be for him to approach me. Unfortunately, there doesn't seem to be the least indication that he is going to pounce on me. So how am I to notice if a spark is leaping over to me or not? Again, I must take a daring step myself.

While Richard avidly reports about his work, which admittedly bores me a little, I approach him inconspicuously. Probably too inconspicuously, since my approach remains unnoticed.

What can I do so that he understands it? I reach for his hand and stroke with my index finger over the tendons on the back of his hand. He really has very manicured large hands. Finally, he stops speaking and looks at me, while I demonstrate my dexterity on him. Curious, I push the sleeve of his sweater up and observe his hairy arm, which I gently stroke with my flat hand. Richard disturbs my exploratory expedition and holds on to my active hand. Disappointed, I look up.

"Malina, it would certainly be the best for us if you go home now."

Ugh! He can't be serious? Not now. Did I go too far again? Naturally I did, but here it's a matter of analyzing my world of feelings. I need more time for my investigations. Absolutely impossible that I drive home now.

"Excuse me, but why?" I ask, bewildered.

"Because I am of the opinion that you need more time."

Yes, that's exactly how I see it. I desperately need more time, and time together with you. That's why it would be dumb of me to end this evening now.

"For what?" I would like to know. I don't assume we both represent the same views in the "matter of time". Thus, an explanation from him couldn't hurt.

"You can't possibly be over Danny. Your dizzy spell earlier leads me to presume that Elisabeth's appearance has affected you more than you would like to admit."

Not right, left me completely cold! Yes indeed! Can I continue now? Come on, give me your arm back!

"Did you know that Danny threw Elisabeth out? That's one of the reasons for her appearance here."

"Danny is no longer together with Elisabeth?" I inquire, bewildered.

Did he have to mention Danny now? That robs me of any stimulus for my investigations. Could Richard be right? Do I really need more time to get over Danny? Anyway, I am beside myself when I just hear his name. That is not good. I am still suffering and almost hadn't noticed it.

"How good is your relationship with Danny and Elisabeth?" I ask Richard with interest.

"Elisabeth and I got along well as children. When she had problems, I was her place to go. That's remained the case until today. However, I am fed up with her continuous intrigue. She was very spoiled by her parents. So she believed she could have everything she wanted. It didn't matter whether it was on a material or a human level. I don't rule out the possibility that she snatched Danny away from you. She likes to play with the feelings of other people."

"That makes no difference to me anymore, Richard. Danny didn't have to let himself be snatched up. That is no excuse."

"Yes, I agree with you," Richard acknowledges to me, "but I want to be honest with you. Danny is really not a bad person. Elisabeth always used his weaknesses to her advantage. They've known each other since their school days and, after Danny's parents passed away, he was no longer good enough for her. When his first musical success came about, her opinion about him seemed to change. A continuous back and forth with the two of them followed. They were together for a while and then they weren't. Nobody could figure it out. Occasionally, he got to know other girls but, as he suddenly appeared on the scene with you, I could have sworn that he was serious. I had never experienced him that way. Anyway, he watched you like a hawk. I simply can't explain his current behavior."

"Whatever. I don't care, since it no longer matters how it came to that."

Richard sympathetically strokes my arm.

"I wish I had met you before Danny!" he says all of a sudden, as if he knew that he had lost the battle for me. And yet I am firmly determined to forget Danny forever. I really must make that clear to him.

"Why do you say that?" I ask, bewildered. "He is no longer important to me. Give me a chance to prove it to you."

Smiling, he bends over to me.

"You're lying to yourself, Malina. You will soon see that. Explore your feelings."

But I just tried to do that. You're not allowing it. I would like to have had your arm back. So?

"It's my fault," he says quietly. "I should not have called again. This evening just confused you even more."

Yes, you can say that. Soon I will know nothing any more. First Richard avoids my advances and then makes it clear that he wants me, but thinks that I want Danny and he should wait until I see whom or what *I* want. I was sure of not wanting Danny anymore, and now I start to fluctuate again, for which Richard is partly responsible.

Probably he is right and it is best that we don't see each other for a while. As it is, I will never calm down inside. I need a firm course. Only my ship is swaying in one direction and then the other. That makes my path more difficult, which I myself no longer know. Man oh man. Nothing will come of this.

Next week I have an appointment with this attorney, Dr. Smith. I want to turn over my completed manuscript, since Danny must bless the content of the book before I can deliver it to my publisher. But there is really no reason for him to be opposed to it. Everything was formulated as he would wish.

Two days later, the last book presentation will take place in a small book store. Afterwards, I will travel to Greenland for a while and visit my parents. Maybe I'll find the necessary peace there to gain clarity about some things.

"You are certainly right," I say to Richard in agreement, "I need more time for myself. It's nice that you are showing so much understanding for me and keeping me from ill-considered actions, which I could regret later."

Richard nods in agreement, but the expression on his face reveals that, at the bottom of his heart, he would like to have heard something different from me. Although he apparently knows better than I that I can say nothing else.

Shortly thereafter, Richard accompanies me to my car.

"It was a very nice evening, Richard. Thanks a lot. May I still call when I feel like it?" I ask uncertainly.

Without answering, Richard reaches for me and pulls me into his arms. For a while, we stand there embracing each other in the dark quiet, until Richard covers my face with his hands and pulls it toward him. If he wants to kiss me, I have to warn him. That speaks against his recently constructed principles. I should first straighten out my feelings before it comes to amorous, technical measures between us.

Has he changed his opinion now? His lips press on mine and, briefly, I hope that his mouth will open and our tongues will meet. But, a moment later, he ends this unplanned action and eases away from me.

Well, maybe it is better this way. I long for physical contact, but I don't know whether Richard should give it to me.

As I drive off from the courtyard, I am almost relieved that my advances with Richard were not crowned with success. His unexpected farewell kiss was nice, but the sizzle was absent.

This news must first be digested

I am sitting across from Dr. Smith, the attorney, and admiring his roomy office for the second time. Even this burly man seems small and lost in it. He is browsing in my manuscript before he talks to me.

"That is all well and good, Miss Bergstroem. I just don't fully understand why you have written the book. Mr. Greyeyes apparently no longer attached importance to the completion and, if I remember correctly, your interest in the project was negligible from the outset. May I ask what motivated you to write the book?"

Clearly he may ask. But I will not answer.

"You know, Mr. Smith, I don't like to write with a knife in my back. The fact that Mr. Greyeyes no longer insisted on adherence to the contract probably first activated my desire to write."

But I didn't want to answer?! How inconsistent!

"Good. In the coming days, I will inform you about Mr. Greyeyes' decision on this manuscript. In case any changes are desired, I will send them to you."

Nothing will be changed! Otherwise, it will land in the trash basket!

"Certainly. Thanks a lot."

Mr. Smith accompanies me to the exit.

No, that won't do! I must make it clear here and now that I will accept no corrections to the manuscript by Danny. He may read it, but nothing more. His interference in my life was so serious that I was not prepared to take it all without resisting. In spite of my disappointment about him, I was able to create a work that examines him without bias. It reflects significant events of his life history and allows an uncensored look at a selected smaller portion of his character.

I also find the "true Danny", whom I got to know, in my book. Consistent, determined, unswerving, sensitive, perceptive, reasonable, witty and talented. All the other experiences gained, which have caused different varieties of love sickness in me, were generously swept under the carpet. Thus, there would be no reason at all for Danny to criticize.

The last weeks have significantly changed my life. I am no more the same person I was before the encounter with Danny. Perhaps I didn't recognize it right away, but now I sense it more clearly. I have learned something from this lesson.

Only one single person decides about my life: namely, I myself. And I certainly will allow nobody to dictate anything to me in the future. Not Lucy, not a "Helen-High Heels", not a Danny or anybody. It has become clear to me that I know best what or how much I can expect of myself. Thus, in the future, my ears will be turned inward, in order to listen to myself.

"Oh, Mr. Smith, please tell Danny that I don't intend to change anything in the manuscript. If it doesn't appeal to him, then I withdraw from the project."

If Mr. Smith responded, I didn't catch anything. My thoughts were making a big leap. I still have an appointment with my doctor and it may be difficult to keep it on time. Although I am certain that everything is in order with my circulation, I followed Richard's advice and underwent a checkup yesterday. Since my last doctor's visit was some time ago, I thought it couldn't hurt to be examined somewhat more thoroughly. So we decided on the whole works. As I thought, without any results. Perfectly healthy. However, a few test results are pending, and I was asked to come in to the office to discuss them today.

I arrive at Dr. Morgan's about a half hour late. Fortunately, the waiting room is empty. A short time later, I am sitting opposite him at his cluttered desk.

Dr. Morgan is a little, gaunt man whom you would not consider to be healthy, since he seems as brittle as old wood. His joints crackle with every move, and his skin is a pale and transparent as parchment paper. All the same, he is a merry, humorous little person who always is ready for a bad joke. This is probably why I chose him for my personal physician. Because it is always casual and relaxed with him. With my constrained nature, he is exactly the right contrast.

"Nice that you did come, Miss Bergstroem. As I presumed, you are overflowing with vitality. Except for your low blood pressure which, because of the overall impression, one can actually ignore."

Well please! That's what I say. Satisfied, I smile at him.

"But, in the future, some things in your life will change, as it seems."

Yes, you can say that again. In the coming days, I will expand my plans for migration to the North Pole. But how does Dr. Morgan know that? Can he read that from my blood tests? Is this life already predetermined?

"How am I to understand that?" I ask, bewildered.

Dr. Morgan smiles and props himself up with his arms folded on the desk.

"I would advise you to spare yourself in the time to come. Cancel all public obligations and try to rest. That's the best for you and your child."

"Pardon? But … I … ugh …"

My child? Is that one of his dumb jokes again?

"To express it with other words, Miss Bergstroem: you are pregnant."

Oh, yes, naturally. I am pregnant. But certainly! If that's all it is. People get pregnant all the time.

I am whaaat? Okay, just don't lose control now. What happened with the birth control? Fine, we did without that. But do I also have to suddenly get pregnant because of that? The probability is extremely small that a whole life will change in a single night. Not small enough. Anyway, not in my case.

Skeptically, I look down and place my right hand on my stomach, which is still as flat as the top of Dr. Morgan's desk.

What do I do now? Pregnant! Me! Am I ready for this? Alone? With no father?

"I hope the news doesn't come to you at an inconvenient time," Dr. Morgan says fretfully.

"But no, by no means. Not at all. Not in the least. Everything is fine. I had thought that. It doesn't really surprise me."

I feel nauseated. Good that I am sitting or this bad news might have knocked my socks off. Now I really need time. And more than an infinite amount, to understand all of this. Unfortunately, I don't have that any more. At most, nine months. Day after tomorrow, I'll catch the next flight to Greenland, as soon as I have this last book presentation behind me.

After I have said good-bye to Dr. Morgan, I decide on an outing to an aquarium. Fish always had a calming effect on me. So I am now sitting in front of a huge fish tank and observing how the bright aquarium inhabitants glide peacefully through the water and rub against the wavy climbing plants.

I don't need to reflect anymore. I have long since made a decision. However, I enjoy the tranquility in the aquarium and let the Neptunian atmosphere take hold of me.

When I finally get home in the late evening, Lucy is awaiting me. She already knows. I had sent her a short bottle post with my cell phone.

Empathetically, she puts her arms around me as we are sitting on the couch. It feels as if she wanted to comfort me. And yet I am uncertain if that is necessary. I always wanted to have children. However, I imagined the how, when and where differently. My problem is not so much that I am standing alone before this large task. I just really always dreamed of a complete family. This doubtlessly includes a father. Unfortunately, this father didn't exactly cover himself with glory. So I would like to remove him from my memory as soon as possible.

"I want the child, only I wish everything had been different," I say, feeling disheartened.

"Don't you think you should inform Danny that you are pregnant?" Lucy interjects, concerned.

Incredulous, I look her in the face.

"By no means! I expect nothing from him. No money or anything else. He just took off, Lucy. Simply disappeared. Do you think the child would mean something to him if he knew it?"

"You can't know that. You should tell him."

Lucy ought to be happy that she has an advance bonus with me. She is suffering terribly because Namid doesn't contact her any more. So I show consideration for her as much as possible. Only at the moment, it is quite difficult not to ring her neck. She knows how much Danny's behavior has hurt me and that I find his jaded sudden disappearance from my life inexcusable.

How can she demand that I tell an immature man, who is only seeking his own pleasure, about his paternity? Here it is not just about me, but about the protection of my child. I am not going to tolerate having it photographed by the newspapers after its birth. It should be able to grow up in a free world, shielded from the public.

That would never be possible in Danny's presence. That is certainly not clear to him. He probably lacks the maturity for that. After all, I have experienced that he is lacking the necessary backbone and is deficient in his sense of responsibility. Otherwise, he wouldn't just simply steal away.

"No, I can't do that! It's best this way."

Astounding how easily the little word "no" moves over my lips. Why was that never possible earlier? Now it goes without a hitch.

On the day before my departure to Greenland, I make myself available for a book presentation, which will be the last one. This time, everything is organized to suit me. Little and quiet. I sign some books and converse lightheartedly with individual readers about my texts. Full of expectation, I am thinking about my parents, my native country and the peace I will again find there. I wish I could have taken Lucy along. A change of scenery would certainly have done her good.

Smiling and lost in thought, I sign the books which are handed me, when, unexpectedly, a hand holds out my new manuscript. Astounded, I look up. Danny is standing opposite me and looking at me approvingly.

"Congratulations! The biography is really a success. I knew that you could do it."

Irritated by his appearance, I look for the fitting words. But I only succeed with a mute look into his eyes.

What does he want here? Did he personally come by just to tell me that? He could have just delivered a message through his attorney.

"Thanks. I hoped you would see it that way," I finally reply. "If it suits you, then I'll turn over the manuscript to the publisher. Of course, I'll hold to the terms of our contract in regard to all points. All royalties will be divided up between us."

"No, no," Danny wards off my remarks. "Those are not owed to me. It is your work alone. And it is really good. Thanks. I wouldn't have thought that you would write like that about me. Not after all that has happened. Even though I will never understand why it all turned out this way. But you certainly had your reasons. I wish you much success with the book!"

Blankly, I hear his words. How does he mean that? What will he never understand? I also had a few questions that have remained unanswered until today. But, before I can reply, the next visitors swarm at me. Danny disappears in the crowd.

How dare he simply act as if he didn't know why everything happened that way. It is obvious. Does he seriously believe that I would be too blind to see through the game? How dumb does he think I am?

My parents pick me up at the little airport of the province where a plane only lands three to four times a week. Overjoyed, I embrace them. Finally home! With the jeep, we drive a good four hours cross country, before we reach the secluded place which was my homeland for so long. There they are. About forty wooden houses in bright colors, which seem lost in this wide landscape. A church, a toy store, and a small school convey the appearance of normality. But the harsh life in this frozen wasteland is full of that which is different. Our house is the next to the last in the second row. Not even a hundred meters away from the foot of the fjord. When the car stops in front of the house and the motor is silent, I hear it. This unbelievable stillness. A light breeze is blowing through my hair. Nothing else. Just gentle quiet and clear air.

An orange-colored sun, which is brushing the border of the horizon, gently warms my face. It is summer, and richly colored flowers are blooming in the grass, which has been growing at most for a few weeks. The summer is short and cool, but vibrant.

"Hello, little sister!" I hear the voice of my brother from the distance.

Namid? He is here? Why did nobody say anything? Reproachfully, I look at my parents. But they just smile at me and disappear with my suitcase in the house.

"Namid, what are you doing here?"

"But little sister, probably the same thing as you. I need time for reflection."

"You? What do you have to reflect about?" I ask spitefully. "Is it clear to you what you have done? In all the years, I have never doubted you. But now, thanks to your behavior, I could go for your throat!"

Fine, my tone didn't have to sharpen like that. But, at this moment, Namid embodies all the unprincipled men of this world. How practical when you can project all of your disappointment onto a single person.

"Tell me, what are you really talking about?" Namid interjects.

I don't have to give him an answer because my mother waves us into the house. With difficulty, I swallow my anger over him. It is not my intention to argue with Namid in front of my parents, whom I haven't seen for so long. I will fight my battle with him later and privately.

Soon we are sitting together at the big table which fills up the whole room. I am sitting at my regular seat, which I have claimed for myself since my childhood. From here, you have the best view into the open kitchen, in which I have so often observed my mother cooking. For dinner, there is canned bread and bright yellow cheese from Denmark. Without any appetite, I reach for an apple.

"So, little sister, tell me what this story is about with Danny Greyeyes. So you moved in with him."

What now? Is this an interrogation? I really had not intended to talk with anybody about me. Not even here do I have my peace!

They all stare at me. My mother gets this curious look, which I inherited from her. That's why I recognize it immediately.

"Do you have a new boyfriend?" she asks, interested. "Why didn't you tell us anything about him?"

My displeasure about Namid starts to grow. Does he want to put me to shame, in order to conceal his own mistakes?

"Because there is nothing to tell, Mum. It was a purely business relationship. Nothing more. He wanted me to write a book about him and I did that. Period!"

So, can we change the subject now?

"But your friend Lucy told me something different. Why don't you admit that you are a couple? It's in all of the newspapers."

You notice that he has been living in isolation for some weeks. Otherwise, he would know about the newest newspaper reports.

"You have no idea! What Lucy told you is history. If you hadn't fled from New York, you could have read about it in any local rag."

My parents are sitting silently next to each other at the table and looking back and forth between Namid and me. A tennis match would not be more suspenseful.

"I didn't know that we were only communicating through the newspaper," Namid growls at me.

"Your type of communication is also new to me. You simply hide yourself here for weeks and I hear nothing from you. I've tried to reach you for days."

My father folds his arms in front of his chest and leans against the back of my mother's chair, while my mother lays her head on his shoulder. They have always done this when there is dissention between Namid and me. They have never interfered. And, since Namid is the more unyielding one, I have always gotten the short end of the stick.

"And what did you want to tell me?" Namid asks, bewildered.

"What I wanted to say to you …? I wanted to say what I think about you. In particular, that you are the most insensitive and coldhearted person that I know."

Including Danny.

"Malina, can you please tell me what you are getting at?"

"You have broken Lucy's heart. I don't care what you do with all your women, but why Lucy of all people?"

Silently, Namid stares through me. I did it! He is silent. I won! For the first time. I knew that that would work. I just don't understand why I needed so many years for this.

Suddenly, Namid stands up and goes off. Astounded, I look after him. Highly perplexing behavior. Maybe I should go after him …?

"Follow him!" my father says in Greenlandic. I jump up immediately and go to the door. My father doesn't talk much. Only when it is really necessary. And then it is usually very important to him. In this case, one should not contradict him. That is an unwritten law in our family to which my mother, Namid, and I always adhere. Thus, I don't know what the consequences would be if you didn't follow his word. Probably there would be none. But just the fact of hearing my father speak is so amazing that it lends enormous meaning to his words.

Namid is already a few steps away, so that I have to run to catch up with him. When I have reached him, we go silently to a little cliff, on which we have sometimes sat together and observed the gulls in the fjord.

The sky this evening is draped with some high and hazy clouds. It is cool, barely over freezing, but it feels warmer. Now, in midsummer, the sun doesn't set completely in the evening and plays with its red colors in the sky. The whole landscape is immersed in an unreal light.

It is unusual for Namid not to talk. We sit together for a time on the cold rock and don't say a word. For me, no new experience. But Namid has inherited the oral fluency of our mother. So I am slowly getting worried.

"I'm sorry. I didn't want to offend you," I say to break the silence.

Bravely, I reach for his hand and press it.

"I don't know what I should say, little sister. Your words have surprised me."

"But how so?"

"Lucy is a terrific woman. It's not just since this one night that I have felt that. But what could I offer her? She is very successful professionally, and I haven't even finished my studies. I hadn't thought I could mean anything to her."

"Now *I* am surprised. You love her."

Why did I never notice? I can hardly believe it.

Both kept their feelings for each other a secret from me, and they don't sense that the other one feels the same.

"Now you think you are not good enough for her. Is that why you retreated here?"

Without answering, Namid looks silently into the distance.

"Go back to her! You were here long enough and have wasted precious time with brooding. She's waiting on a sign from you."

Why are men so complicated? Instead of simply talking to her, he buries his pain and just ponders here alone.

"Okay. Maybe you are right. I will talk to her. And what's with you?" he asks. "Do you want to waste *your* precious time now with contemplation?"

Actually, that's what I intended, yes. Does he want to hint at something with this question?

"Everything is different with me. There's nothing more to salvage, Namid."

"Obviously! And why?" he inquires subtly.

My pain is catching up with me again. Can't we talk about something else? Namid is not my girlfriend. Actually, I would rather not confide in him. His arm stretches around my shoulder and pulls me to him.

"Come on, tell me about it!" he pushes.

Apparently there's no way around it. Curiosity is an epidemic in this family and can hardly be overcome. Namid is also influenced by it.

"I don't know why it all turned out this way. At first, I was floating on pink clouds and everything seemed perfect. Until his ex-girlfriend called and made it clear that Danny would not come back to me and I should forget him. A few weeks later, I saw him together with her. That's the whole story."

"Is that really everything?"

Why does he ask that? Can you tell by looking that I am pregnant? Unsure, I peer at my stomach. It registers with Namid right off, and he turns his upper body in my direction.

"Are you pregnant?"

Rolling my eyes, I am irritated about myself and my ill-considered gesture toward my stomach. So much for my wish to consider everything in peace. When my mother learns about this, any sort of peace is down the drain. She will ask me to look for a suitable father for the child. She might have given me a modern education, considering the circumstances in Greenland. But she could never accept my bringing a child into the world unmarried. It's going to be hard work to make it clear that I've decided to be a single mother and no suitable father is in sight.

"Does he know that? He just left you stranded pregnant? I will beat the hell out of him."

"No. He doesn't know anything. It wouldn't interest him either. The life that he leads is one without obligations, which offers neither me nor a child sufficient room."

"I understand. Nonetheless, I think he has a right to know about it. You shouldn't keep it from him that he's becoming a father."

"When I'm in New York again, I'll give him a good talking to. I should have done that when we met in your apartment."

Now this protective syndrome is budding out in him. He has never realized that I have grown up in the meantime and he should direct his attention at other things: for instance, at Lucy.

"Thank you for your concern, but it is really not appropriate in this case. It is not necessary for you to confront Danny. I'll get along without him."

"If you think so. But you should talk with Mum and Dad about it."

I was afraid of that. So much for my eagerly anticipated peace. I should have stayed in New York. I'm simply not prepared for discussions with my mother.

"Well that's fine."

Which father should it be?

Naturally it turned out as I thought. When my parents learned that I am pregnant, the debate got going. A whole five days. I am totally exhausted. Now I am sitting on my rock overhang and staring into the glistening water. Namid took off and travelled back to New York. I understand my mother. She found the man of her life, namely my father. Thus, she never faced the decision of having to raise a child alone. If she lived in New York, she would know that it is nothing unusual to be an unmarried, single mother. But she lives at the edge of the world. How could she have formed an open-minded opinion?

My father stayed out of the dispute between my mother and me. Very smart of him. If it hadn't involved me, I would have done the same.

Today she asked me in all seriousness to speak with Phil. She informed me that he was available again and had regularly inquired about me the last few years. If she has told him a single word about me, I could consider future sanctions toward her.

For instance, I could turn off the flow of information about me. Naturally I am aware that she couldn't stand it more than twenty four hours to hear nothing of me. But I must be able to count on her to treat everything I entrust her with as "top secret" and not discuss it with my ex.

Unfortunately, she simply doesn't want to understand that I do not need a husband, just for the sake of the child. But I did let her talk me into a discussion with Phil, just to finally have my peace. Five days can be very long, when the focus is continuously on the same subject.

I have encountered Phil numerous times in the last days. In such a tiny place, that simply cannot be avoided. However, I haven't exchanged more than two words with him. But really that was not my intention. Until today. If I can finally silence my mother in this way, I am ready to make this sacrifice.

I ordered Phil to my rock. Everyone here knows that it is my place where I can always be found. From here, I have contrived all of my schemes. The plan to go to New York matured here. Now my rock will be the witness to the next decision, whether my child will grow up with or without a father.

Calmly, I sit on the rock overhang and wait for Phil. Naturally, the clocks move more slowly here than elsewhere, and yet I've been waiting over an hour. Could it be that he has forgotten? I can't deny that his lack of punctuality suits me just fine. I don't have the least desire for a discussion with him. What is there to talk about? After such a long time.

I notice steps that are approaching. My God, what am I doing here? Phil and me, that is over.

Never in my life could I get involved with him again. I have to clarify that immediately.

"Well, I'm just in time!" I hear a voice behind me say. Horrified, I turn around and see Danny coming toward me. But that can't be! How does he know …? What does he know …? How did he find me? Stunned, I get up from my rock and stand as motionless as a monument. As Danny stands in front of me, he angrily grabs my arm.

"Damn it, why didn't you say anything? I can't believe it! You are pregnant by me and travel to Greenland without a word. Why don't you talk with me about it? Damn! I want to know why you wanted to hide it from me?"

Surprised by Danny's indignant behavior, along with the fact of meeting him here, I am completely astonished. "I don't know why you completely vanished from my life," he continues his monologue, "but one thing is hopefully clear to you: I will not allow you to pawn off some perfect stranger as the father of my child. I am the father! So you will marry me!"

These last words shake me up. What is he imagining? I'm not going to marry any man who will be unfaithful at the next best opportunity. He has really miscalculated this one.

"What gives you the idea that I would like to marry you?" I reply to him indignantly.

Pooh! Just because I am pregnant by him, he doesn't need to put on airs like Napoleon at the Battle of Waterloo.

"Do you think that I will just accept you letting yourself be paired off with your ex by your mother?"

"How do you know that? How did you find me anyway?"

"Damn, that doesn't matter at all! Tomorrow you will fly back to New York with me. I have already organized everything."

"How dare you go over my head to make decisions for me! I'm not about to fly anywhere with you. I am staying here! And for as long as I like! In the case that I should marry – which is not at all certain – then *I* will decide who and when."

Incensed, I grab my jacket, which is still lying on the cliff, and run off. My path leads me past the boats over a small hill, behind which my father's huskies are lying in the evening sun. They are probably the only ones who are pleased about the coming onset of winter, when they will finally be spanned in front of a sleigh.

I sit down to stroke them. I'm sure I have Namid to thank for Danny's appearance here. As soon as I am back, he's going to be in for it. If he only knew the harm he has caused. Danny has completely gone wild. I never would have expected that he would react to the news of my pregnancy by flaring up. Something isn't right. Why did he leave me for this Elisabeth if not out of egotism?

I don't know how long I have spent with the dogs when I notice Danny on the hill. He sat down in the grass and has been observing me with the animals. It is clear that the most reasonable thing would be to talk to him about everything calmly. But it is so hard to approach him.

After a while, I get up my courage and climb up to him. Silently, I sit down opposite him. In the sustained evening twilight, his deep black eyes seem like a dark dungeon, into which I could sink any moment. His dimples are pulling me deeper and deeper. Can it be that all my feelings for him are being rekindled at this short moment? I knew from the beginning that these frown lines could become an incalculable danger for me. Now I would like to be consistent, but this desperate facial expression causes me to doubt my position of having decided correctly.

I should have told him. It was wrong not to have informed him about my pregnancy. Whatever he has done. He should have learned it from me.

"You are right. I made a wrong decision," I admit, repentant. "I should have informed you about it. I am sorry." With an agreeable nod, he confirms that my words have reached him. "Of course, you can visit our child at any time. I won't get in the way. But I can't marry you. Too much has happened for that."

Hopefully, he doesn't notice that my mouth is spouting out something different than what I think. Actually, I would rather fling my arms around his neck, since he has made the long journey to me. It is shattering to have to decide against going back to him. But it is the most reasonable thing. I could never get over a new disappointment.

"I understand," Danny answers and looks at me longingly.

With a desire to be forgiving, I reach out my hand, which he grabs immediately. While his warm hand strokes the back of my hand, I struggle against the increased pounding in my chest. I would like to pounce on him, rip the clothes from his body, and devour him like food for the gods. It's good that the cold hinders me from such reckless behavior. On this bright evening, the temperatures have dipped right under freezing; so I get up from the cold ground and pull Danny up with my hand.

"Come on, let's walk for a bit. I'll show you my homeland," I suggest.

Hand in hand, we walk over the fresh green of the grass surfaces. The orange colored twilight makes the whole area appear unique, and the houses of the little place merge in color with the landscape. I sense that it will be hard for me to let Danny depart again. His presence feels good. His hand feels good. Simply everything is good when he is with me.

Dim light penetrates the window when, after a few hours, we return to my parents' house. They just went to bed and left a small candle burning on the table for us. Softly, with the candle, we sneak into the room that I normally must share with Namid. We'll spend the coming night together in this room. Since the house only has two rooms, there is no other alternative.

Danny follows me silently, as he has done during the whole walk. For the first time, I succeeded in letting my thoughts wander with Danny. Something that hasn't worked out since my arrival. If nothing else on account of the many disputes with my mother. In the last hours, I have found peace and, of all things, with the person who robbed me of it before. I wish I had an explanation for it. His presence gives me strength. Why?

"It is beautiful here," Danny says softly. "So secluded and peaceful. I've been longing for this."

From the other corner of the room, I look questioningly in his direction. Is that still the same Danny? What is going on inside him? Thoughtfully, I take off my clothes down to my underwear and place them neatly folded on the floor. Danny's confused look concerning my natural behavior surprises me. Did he want to go to bed in his clothes? Quickly, I scamper into the big bed and disappear under the blanket.

"Do you want to remain standing that way the whole night?" I ask him blatantly. "Come on!"

By candlelight, he steps to the bed and sits down on the edge. Would he rather sleep on the imaginary sofa? That could be an uncomfortable night for him.

"I don't know if that is a good idea," he answers with mixed feelings.

What a dumb observation! As if he had another choice. There are no other sleeping possibilities for him. That must have occurred to him. Unperturbed, I reach for his arm and pull him up to me.

"Danny, there is only this one bed. So, if you don't want to spend the whole night on the chair, you should come to bed. Come on," I ask him. "Raise your arms."

Well-behaved, he does what I say and lets me pull the sweater over his head. It would have been better if I had not gotten carried away with this action, since the view of his naked upper body leads to an appetite for more, difficult to restrain. I'm afraid my lustful looks are not unobtrusive enough. Better if I look in another direction. Quickly I turn my face to the wall.

"Malina," he whispers into my ear. His hand presses my head back gently, so that we look directly into each other's eyes. "Tell me that you love me and that everything was just a mistake! Please!"

His comment confuses me. What was supposed to be a misunderstanding, in his opinion? What happened with Elisabeth? My book about him? My pregnancy kept secret from him? Or that I can hardly contain myself and may transform myself into an open box of chocolates. If he nibbles on me now, I won't be able to stop it. Even if

I wanted to. I will melt. He wants for me to love him. But I do. That's the problem. If I only knew how I could fight against it.

I simply can't reply to him. He's demanding too much of me. *He* was the one who suddenly disappeared from the scene. I am not the one to confess my love, but he is the one.

"Please say something! I need certainty," he begs.

"Yes," I say unexpectedly. Simply "yes". I don't know what I want to express with this yes, but now it is out. The rest he'll have to imagine. Any more won't work.

Agitated, his eyes examine me. This crackling between us is so loud that I'm afraid my parents can hear it. Either he puts something on here on the spot or my hands will start wandering. I decide on wandering, which seems much more exciting. Hesitating, I touch his shoulders and let my fingers wander down his arm.

His glance follows my hand, which gently strokes the hairs of his arms. Everything is there again. This passion and my burning desire. But I have forgotten nothing of all this. The pain is burned into my memory. It was this call from Elisabeth and the humiliation of seeing them together right after that. But now I can't stop myself. I want him now for myself! One last time! This one night!

My fingers circle around his navel without any inhibition. I don't know what they are doing there. They are operating on their own. All of a sudden, they slide deeper and open his trouser button. Skillfully, I succeed in pulling down the zipper before he removes my hand from the danger zone.

"You know very well that I can't resist you," he mumbles and pulls my head toward him. Gently, his lips touch my cheek and come closer to my mouth. Finally, he kisses me and presses himself against me.

"I do not want to lose you again," he says unexpectedly and passionately kisses my neck.

I would very much like to ask what he means by that. But that would ruin all of the romance. On the other hand, I know myself. I wouldn't be able to think of anything else and would be seeking an answer which only Danny can give.

"But you never had lost me. I had lost you. Why do you twist the facts?"

Bewildered, Danny lets go of me and looks at me with his thoughtful, dimpled glance.

"What's the point of that?" he asks, irritated. "Why are you saying something like that?"

"Because it's the truth."

"Which truth do you mean then? The one you presented before or after your disappearance?"

The tone of his voice hurts me. Why does he portray it as if I were the one who wanted to leave him? Clever number.

"What are you talking about anyway? I didn't disappear, but you did!" I defend myself, incensed.

"Admit that you gave in to the flattery of Richard Daniels, and so you didn't care about me anymore!"

What nerve! I would never have suspected so much audacity from him. I can hardly outdo that.

"Richard Daniels has nothing at all to do with all that."

"That's why you were whispering sweet nothings with him in public a short time later. Don't tell me otherwise. I noticed right off that something was brewing between you."

Always these allegations. He simply can't leave it alone.

"If you absolutely want to believe that, I can't prevent you from it. Elisabeth also seemed more important to you. I just don't understand why you gave up again so quickly. You really made a perfect couple."

His look darkens noticeably.

"I think it was a mistake to come here!" he replies. "It'll be best if I leave right away in the morning. We should just end this fruitless conversation. Everything has been said between us."

Logical! It has all been said. Just not the essential. But what does that matter? The result remains the same. In the end, he left me, before it really got started. And now he distorts everything while putting me to shame. If he feels better that way, he can portray it that way, for all I care. My pain remains the same.

Shortly thereafter, Danny grabs his bedding and makes up a bed on the carpet. If that's what he wants. He can suffer the back ache tomorrow himself.

Before I am really awake, Danny is hastily packing his things. Most likely, his night was lousier than mine was. But what do I care? Let him disintegrate into air so that peace returns here. The events of the last evening have agitated me such that I can begin with fighting the heartache anew. It would really have been best if he had not joined me. Now everything has become more complicated. My heart is bleeding to death, and nothing can stop this bleeding, unless Danny could be my bandage. And I thought I was over the worst. Fatal mistake. Crap!

I could box his ears for his behavior. Why doesn't he possess the integrity to admit his mistake? He only needed to tell me that he was sorry and I would have been prepared to forgive him yesterday. Under these circumstances, however, I must let him go, if I want to maintain even a bit of dignity.

Without a further word, he leaves the house at the crack of dawn and roars away in his vehicle. Standing at the window, I look after him and struggle with my tears. Only now do I notice my parents behind me. They have observed everything. My mother puts her arms around me to comfort me.

"You should go after him," she advises me unexpectedly.

"But Mum, he didn't even have the courage to explain to me why he left me. Now he's leaving me for the second time. And, again, I don't know the reason for it."

"Didn't he tell you anything?"

"No, what should he have said to me?"

"He told us yesterday that he was in the hospital because he had a car accident. You had never inquired about him and, after his release, you had moved out of his house. He learned from the media that you had told the press in front of your house that you were never together with him. And, a short time later, there were rumors that you were involved with a Richard Daniels. His portrayal of things is completely different from yours. You two should have talked about it."

"What are you telling me …?"

He was in the hospital? A car accident? But … that explains everything! Now I understand. And this Elisabeth cleverly twisted the story. That snake!

"He didn't tell me anything about that. I knew nothing about it. And I thought he wanted to have nothing more to do with me."

"He thought the same about you."

Now everything is becoming clear. His behavior yesterday evening and all his comments I couldn't make any sense of.

"Dad, please give me the car keys. I have to go after him!"

"I'll drive you," my father decides, while he puts on his jacket and hurries out of the house.

Puzzled about his decision, I follow him and sit on the passenger side of the jeep. Hopefully, he still knows where the gas pedal is. Usually, he creeps along almost at a walking speed. That could cost valuable time. With squeaking tires, he speeds off so that I am pushed into the seat. Wow! Where did he learn that? My father seldom shows emotions. But the core under the hard shell is super soft. He takes things to heart, even though he doesn't talk about it.

After a good half hour, we can make out Danny's vehicle in the distance. With the jeep, we are making better time in this terrain than Danny with his little rental car. But when he reaches the crossing ahead of us that leads to the well constructed main road, we'll have no more chance of catching up. My father knows this, and so he is driving at the very limit. But no chance! We won't make it. Then suddenly my father veers from the normal route and drives through the middle of the terrain. Hopefully, he knows what he is doing. The gravel road was bumpy, but what comes now turns my stomach. Desperately, I hold on tight inside the car, but I'm being shaken up like a cocktail. Now I notice that the street makes a bend, and we are catching up a good bit through this daring measure. But we are not going to make it. A hill cuts off our path. The gravel road is directed around this hill before it meets the main street. We won't reach anything with the jeep any more. Only one chance remains for me: I have to climb over this hill as fast as I can. Maybe I'll catch him behind it.

"Daddy, stop immediately!"

On the spot, I jump out of the car and run over the hill. Danny's car is just bending around the corner, when I blindly hop onto the street, to place myself in the way. Sliding over the gravel, it comes to a stop right before my knees. Foaming with rage, he lunges out of the car.

"Are you completely bonkers? You can't just jump in front of a car! What if I hadn't been able to brake in time?"

Without reacting to his insults, I hurry over to him, agitated, and reach for his hand.

"Danny, I didn't know anything about your having an accident on that evening. I just learned about it."

Curtly, he pulls his arm away.

"Why are you telling me this now? Do you think I didn't know that you were putting something over on me?"

"But that is not true! On that evening, when you didn't come back, this Elisabeth called me and told me I should forget you, since you were with her. She told me nothing about your accident. I thought you were together with her again. How could I know that she was lying to me?"

"You did a fine job of thinking that one up. Your brother, your parents and you are in cahoots with each other. Is that why you let me get you pregnant? Is it about money? Is that what you want from me?"

Money? What would I do with his money? He should know that this claim is far-fetched. What can I say so that he finally understands?

"I don't need any money! I need you! Our child needs you! If you don't believe me, then ask your Elisabeth. If it weren't for her, it never would have come to this."

"Now you're making it very easy for yourself. I thought you were different. Honest and genuine. Probably I assumed too much about you."

Surprisingly, my father stands between us and grabs Danny by the shoulders.

"She loves you! That is her only mistake. Your mouth speaks before your head thinks. That is your mistake."

For a moment, both men look each other in the eye, until my father turns from Danny and pulls me away by the arm. As we step over the hill, I look around toward Danny one last time. He is still standing unchanged at the same place, and thoughtfully looks back at us.

A Bath with Consequences

Even though I really planned to spend the coming weeks with my parents, I suddenly could no longer bear this isolation. I felt drawn back to the city. I needed people and business goings on around me. Diversion.

Phil and I had had our talk, however. Well, my mouth was "off" and he "spoke". In the process, I learned that Madleine – my and his Ex – left him, to start a new life in another city. Phil is an original plant. He would never have accompanied her. You can't transplant an old tree. Even if he is not so old. But he is a tree, nonetheless. He is one that wants to become old. Namely there where his roots are. City life is not for him.

I'm standing with my parents on the grounds of the little airport, to tell them farewell. It is hard to have to go again. But, with the present situation, it would be even harder to stay. Besides, I would like to take care of some things in New York. Or let's say I have continuously thought about what all I could see to in New York, so that I can take care of something, only in order to take care of something. I desperately need some variety.

Lucy and Namid want to pick me up at the airport in New York. Honestly, I think it's great that they are a couple. But must they appear as a couple before my very eyes right now? Couldn't one of them pick me up from the airport first and the other then arrive by chance?

Okay, okay, okay … I know that is terribly egotistical of me. I'm honestly glad for them. Only that does not distract me from my problems with Danny.

This time, my father squeezes me especially long to say good-bye. I almost have the feeling he doesn't want to let go of me at all. It hasn't escaped me that what happened with Danny and me concerns him. Not that he would have said something more about it. He is persistently silent about this matter. As in all other areas of life.

When he pulled me away from Danny on the gravel road after he had given him these four expressive sentences as advice, my father didn't say another word, not on the drive back or in the next forty eight hours. Naturally I know him well enough to realize that this is not alarming. This can occur without any worries plaguing him. Nonetheless, I would like to have known his thoughts. I know that things strike his attention that remain hidden to others. That certainly could have been useful to me. In one way or the other.

Now we stand on the asphalt of the airport grounds for a few seconds and hug each other silently. Departure ceremonies of this type suit me best. You don't have to intensely search for the right words, which don't make the departure any easier. Instead, you can say farewell silently in the arms of the other person.

"Some paths are long and weary. But not unreachable. Trust your feelings!"

"Thanks, Dad. I'll do that."

What does that mean now? Could you please be somewhat clearer?

Shortly after the landing in New York, I am about five pounds lighter. All the contents of my stomach – aside from my attached organs – are located in the toilet on board. About a dozen times, I have thrown up, but now I seem to be doing well, as if nothing had happened. I don't exactly know whether an illness from traveling or maybe the pregnancy have put pressure on my well being or my stomach. But now all is well again. It's that simple. There's nothing more in there that could come out of my stomach.

Lucy and Namid are standing entangled in the arrival hall and haven't even noticed me. Pooh! No, it doesn't matter to me. Why should it? It's great that the two of them have found each other. I am happy for them. Honestly. But, right now, I have no use for a cooing pair of lovers. That reminds me of my own heartache.

"Malina, here we are!" Lucy calls to me.

Oh, wouldn't have noticed at all. Nice that they did discover me, however.

Weak but pleased to have finally arrived, I plop into Lucy's car a short time later, and the two of them drive me home. Now I'm longing for an extended bath. Afterwards, I will slip into my woolen nightgown, put on my thick socks and nestle under my woolen blanket on the couch. But the summer temperatures could ruin my fun with this.

Hardly have we arrived at home when Lucy takes me aside, while Namid resolutely keeps going toward the kitchen. Is there anything special? I might be a little famished already.

"Thank you, Malina. For everything."

What does she mean? Yes, yes, it's fine. What is there to eat?

"If it weren't for you, nothing would have happened so fast with Namid and me."

Why? What did I do? Is it my doing that the two of them constantly skirmish around in front of my eyes?

"Even though I do resent it a bit that you revealed my emotions to Namid. But, on the other hand, he probably wouldn't have had the courage otherwise to make me a marriage proposal."

Huh!

"I think I have something in my ear. What was your last sentence?"

"We're getting married!" she repeats her statement excitedly.

Sooo! They're getting married. It's about time. After so many days. Others get married after a few hours.

"Congratulations! How nice for you two. I'm very pleased."

Can I please be alone now? I need a little space for my depression phase that is just beginning.

"You will certainly understand that I need a relaxing bath after my long trip, before I concern myself with your marriage plans."

Why does she seem so alarmed when she looks at me?

"But that's not possible," Lucy flares up in dismay.

"Naturally that will work," I correct her. "That is very simple. I go into the bath, turn on the water faucet and climb into the warm water. Who can argue with that?"

Is there something wrong? Why does she look so helpless? I just can't show any consideration for that now. I have to get in the tub and ponder about my life in peace.

A quarter of an hour later, I glide into the warm water. A short, liberating sigh and I am basically far away. I dream of warm ice floes without ice, of baby seals and a little house with a garden at the North Pole. Whispering at the door brings me out of my dreams. Can't you just swim away in peace? If I should ever find my peace of mind again in this country, then I promise to never get involved with a man again. Let's shake on it.

After my pledge, I stand up and reach for the towel. Surprisingly, the bathroom door is pushed open and Danny tumbles in. From shock over this unexpected reunion in the bathroom, with me in the buff, I drop my towel into the draining water. For lack of anything else, the shower curtain has to serve as a cover for the naked facts.

"I can't wait any longer," he starts talking wildly, without noticing what an awkward position has shameless march into my bathroom has put me in.

Lucy stands behind Danny in the doorway and makes a helpless gesture, while she gives me an imploring look. She tries to give me some sign that I can't decipher, until Namid pulls her away and closes the door from outside. Now we are alone. Danny, the shower curtain, and I.

"I have to talk with you. Please come out," Danny demands thoughtlessly.

I would like to. I am missing something very basic.

"Could you please hand me a towel first," I ask him and point to a stack of towels in front of his nose.

Only now does he seem aware of my situation. Perturbed, I pull the curtain around me tighter. His hand reaches for a towel, but he doesn't refrain from looking at me.

Fine. Now you just have to give it to me. That can't be so hard. So why doesn't he do it?

Impatiently, I reach out my hand in the hope that he would give me the desired object. But now he puts the towel away again, snatches my hand and pulls me foreword. I lose my balance and fall into his arms – shower curtain and all. Wrapped up like a mummy, I thrash about for my life.

"What are you doing? Let go of me right now!"

Laughing, Danny lets me slowly glide to the floor.

"You don't need to hide anything from me. I know every centimeter of your body."

That might be, but that was before you broke up with me in Greenland. Now the matter looks completely different. Since I am completely buttoned up, inside as well as outside.

"I thought there is nothing more to discuss between us?" I ask him flippantly. "Or did you just want to pick up my account number? After all, I'm only interested in your money." This time, my provocation doesn't seem to ruffle Danny at all. Smiling, he remains silent. "You wanted to talk to me?" I continue. "About what? About my lies, which you look for in each of my statements? Maybe you would like to negotiate visiting rights for the child. We can talk about that. But only if the payment is right."

"Listen, Malina, everything you said is true. I don't understand how I could be so blind. Elisabeth lied to us both. She was supposed to inform you about my accident, on my behalf. When it happened, she was there, since I had just left her apartment. Shortly after I drove out of the parking space, a drunken driver rammed me. I had two broken ribs and a few bruises, but nothing serious.

But the emergency physician insisted on taking me to the hospital. And yet I only wanted to get back to you. That with Elisabeth was long over. Only she simply didn't want to accept it. In no case was she going to stand between us. That's why I went to her that evening, to finally make it clear that it is over. If only I had listened to you and explained everything before. Then it wouldn't have gone so far. You said one should never put something off. How right you were."

"I didn't say that, but my father did."

"Your father is very wise. When you jumped in front of my car, I was beside myself with rage. I could not believe and did not want to believe what you were saying. With his comment, your father gave me a piece of his mind. Sometimes, I'm a little too hot-headed."

You can certainly say that.

"Maybe you can work a bit on this weakness," I say with a playful smile.

Danny's left eyebrow moves upward. His arms are like a boa when it overpowers its prey. They draw up tighter around me, to devour me any moment.

"How do you know about Elisabeth's deception?" I ask inquisitively.

"I called her on the day after my departure from Greenland. When she noticed that I had uncovered her tasteless intrigue, she didn't deny it anymore."

"And what is with you and Elisabeth?"

"Nothing at all! Shortly after I was released from the hospital, she hung on to me. We went out together a few times. But there was nothing more than that. You have to believe me! Okay, she tried it one time, but then I threw her out of my house. Since then, there has been absolute silence. Two weeks ago, Richard and I talked with each other. He confided in me what feelings he has for you. I admit that it bothered me for a time. But it opened my eyes and made it clear to me that I should fight for you and you don't love him. He expressed the assumption that you might be pregnant. Without an apparent reason, you had a sudden feeling of faintness two times."

"Then you didn't learn about it from Namid?" I ask, relieved.

"No," he answers, smiling. "However, your brother did look me up and was very upset. I think he wanted to fight with me. But, after a few beers together, he explained where I could find you. When I arrived in your village, I was just able to prevent the absurd meeting with this Phil. I made it clear to your mother that I am the father of the child. So then she cancelled the appointment with your ex. Well, yes, and you know the rest. I learned from your brother when you are coming back. I really wanted to pick you up at the airport, but your girlfriend and your brother thought it better for me to wait for you here."

That's why Lucy was so nervous when I said I'd like to take a bath. Danny was already there the whole time. That blows my mind.

"Now I also know that your friend Lucy gave up her prize. She was the real winner of the dinner. And you didn't have the vaguest idea who I was anyway. That's why you were so unsure of yourself at the interview with *Star Magazine*," he recalls, grinning.

"That was rather embarrassing!" I admit openly.

"No, it wasn't that at all. You were just likeable. Your genuineness was apparent to everyone right off. From the first second on, I was infatuated with you. I don't want this underhandedness of Elizabeth to destroy everything I've searched for so long. Could you imagine forgiving me?" he asks me cautiously.

I could imagine that. But what is there to forgive, if Elisabeth was pulling the strings in which Danny and I got caught? The question had to be whether I could forgive Elisabeth, and I could take that into consideration, if that should be of use to anyone.

Danny's turning up here surprised me. After all that had happened, I was banking on a solo for two. Danny, as a possible third member in the league, was being separated out bit by bit. Even though it was with reluctance. For I still had a ray of hope based on the disguised prophecy my father conveyed on my departure. Even though I didn't completely understand the coded message, I sensed what he wanted to tell me with it. A difficult path can still be conquered. With this, did he mean the path that Danny and I have set out on?

"Under certain circumstances, I would be ready for that," I answer his question, impishly.

"So? And these would be?"

Doubtlessly, I am in a situation, in which I could make demands without restraint. Some interesting little things would occur to me, which could make life for a woman rather pleasant. But, since I am not a typical woman (which is naturally not true, since I have determined the opposite in the last weeks. But this can be overlooked), my demands will be minor or almost minor.

"No more pre-judging. You ask me first before you start to form an opinion. Although it was definitely amusing to be taken for nineteen." My grin causes Danny to take me more firmly in his arms. Hopefully, he doesn't forget from pure exuberance that he's cutting off my air. "No more unnecessary public appearances. I prefer to live incognito, as much as possible. Which of course doesn't mean that you should give up your profession. It would be nice if you could keep me out of it. To the extent possible. Our child should be able to grow up free and without scrutiny."

"And that can certainly be arranged. I've long since realized that life in a goldfish bowl doesn't suit you. Your wish in this matter is not ill-timed for me. Peace is exactly what I am longing for."

*That could have come from me. How about a house
at the North Pole?*

"By the way, I sold my house. It had no soul,"
he adds, smiling. "And, after you moved out, it
seemed so empty. If you like, then we'll move to
Greenland to your parents or ..."

"... the North Pole?" I end his sentence quizzically.

"As far as I am concerned," he says and
laughs.

***

Naturally, we didn't move to the North Pole, but simply went out of the city into the country. Danny bought us a beautiful little house that I furnished with all kinds of odds and ends, which gave it more soul. In my opinion, this made it terribly cozy.

I'm just sitting with Lucy in our kitchen, while Jason and Jill are playing in the garden. Lucy became pregnant shortly after me, and Jason beheld the light of the world a few weeks later than our daughter Jill. They understand each other splendidly. Just like Namid and Danny understand each other extremely well. Namid gave up his permanent studies and started playing music together with Danny. In the meantime, rather successfully.

Lucy and I have written a book together about a newly discovered culture, which she encountered during a recent excavation. It's selling almost as well as the biography that I wrote about Danny. Public appearances don't make much difference any more, but I try to avoid them as much as possible. Today I am a good friend of Richard Daniels, and my contact with his mother is very warm. I place a high value on this. Fortunately, my friendship with Richard doesn't matter to Danny, which is likely related to the fact that Richard is now happily married.

Lucy and I are busy with the preparations for the buffet. This evening, we are all getting together again. Even Elisabeth will be part of the group. Her new lover is a known actor, whose name I will never remember. But I don't need to anyway. After all, it is just a matter of time when she will change over to the next admirer. She never can stand more than a few months with one man. By now, I find her to be okay, even though I think her choice of the color red for clothes is questionable.

By the way, I have never found my peace again, in spite of everything. The last six years were just too turbulent, and Jill was partly responsible for this. But I have regretted nothing. I enjoy every moment with Danny and Jill, and, nowadays, a life at the North Pole would be much too lonely.

Leseprobe:

„Kein Sex mit einem Millionär"
von
Sabine Richling

1

„Mein Gott, was redest du wieder für dummes Zeug!", knallt mir mein Mann um die Ohren, während wir mit seinen Geschäftsfreunden in einem Restaurant zu viert am Tisch sitzen und über Politik reden. Gähn! Ich habe mir erlaubt, meinen Senf dazuzugeben, eine kleine Anmerkung zu machen, als ich merkte, dass mein werter Gatte falsch informiert ist. Aber erneut ist es ihm gelungen, seine eigenen Unzulänglichkeiten zu verbergen, indem er mich als latent verblödet darstellt. Peinlich berührt hüstelt Herr Hühnerbein in die Serviette, auch seine Frau popelt mit der Gabel im Fleisch herum und überlegt, wie sie die gute Stimmung retten kann. Komisch, dass mein Daniel solche Überlegungen nie anstellt, schließlich bringt er uns regelmäßig in solch eine Lage, in der man gerne vor Schmach im Boden versinken möchte. Ich überlege, mir eine Tüte über den Kopf zu ziehen, um mir damit kurzfristig das Gefühl zu geben, nicht hier zu sein.

Seine Beleidigung zu kommentieren, erspare ich mir, immerhin haben wir uns gerade ausreichend zum Gespött des Abends gemacht. Das bedarf keiner Fortsetzung.

„Entschuldige", sage ich leise und lege mein Besteck beiseite. Mir ist der Appetit vergangen.

„Wenn du es nicht besser weißt, halte dich aus dem Gespräch heraus", tritt Daniel nach.

Jetzt bin ich still und möchte meinem Gemahl gerne meine Roulade ins vorlaute Mundwerk stopfen, da ich sie ohnehin nicht mehr essen werde. Doch ich halte mich zurück und schlucke meine Wut herunter.

„Sagen Sie, Herr Hartmann", geht Frau Hühnerbein dazwischen, „wohin fahren Sie eigentlich dieses Jahr in den Urlaub?"

Geschickt hat sie das Thema gewechselt und die Lage entschärft.

Da erwacht Daniel zu neuem Leben, denn über Urlaube redet er gern. Als hätte es seine Entgleisung nicht gegeben, gerät er in feurige Ekstase.

„Dieses Jahr haben wir fünf Reisen geplant. Im Frühjahr werden wir wieder eine Kreuzfahrt machen, diesmal auf dem Mittelmeer", antwortet er voller Inbrunst.

„Oh", entfährt es Frau Hühnerbein, „das ist ja großartig.

„Ja, aber dieser Trip ist nicht unser Haupturlaub, den werden wir in Südafrika verbringen, nicht wahr, Leonie?" Er lächelt mich an und stößt mir seinen Ellenbogen gegen den Oberarm. „Da freuen wir uns besonders drauf."

„Klar", sage ich und verstumme sogleich wieder. Ich möchte nicht noch einmal zurechtgewiesen werden, weil ich in seinen Augen Müll rede.

„Du hast diese Reise doch gebucht, sag ruhig auch mal was dazu."

„Ja, später, ich muss mal aufs Klo", erwidere ich gereizt und erhebe mich. Ich hänge mir meine Handtasche über die Schulter und erwäge, einfach zu gehen. Stattdessen steuere ich die Waschräume an, ich Feigling! Ich weiß nicht, warum er mich ständig bloßstellen muss. Natürlich habe ich die Reise nicht gebucht, sondern er. Ich habe keinen blassen Schimmer, wohin es genau geht und welche Hotels er für uns ausgesucht hat. Ich hasse es zu verreisen! Meine Heimat ist mir lieb und teuer und ebenso mein Hobby. Ich male. Seit meiner Jugend beschäftige ich mich mit der Malerei und könnte den ganzen Tag nichts anderes tun. Warum soll ich in die weite Welt fahren, wenn ich mit dem, was mir das Leben hier bietet, äußerst zufrieden bin? Daniel möchte am liebsten von einem Kontinent zum nächsten springen, und das mehrmals im Jahr. Vielleicht rennt er vor irgendetwas davon, ist auf der Suche nach einer Offenbarung. Bloß in der Ferne wird er sie nicht finden. Eine Exkursion in sein übertriebenes Ego könnte ihm guttun. Womöglich stößt er dabei mal auf sich selbst und erkennt, was er für ein selbstverliebter Blödmann ist.

Er war nicht immer so. Früher war er mal nett, damals – vor langer Zeit. Wir haben für eine Modekette gearbeitet, waren Kollegen, besser gesagt, Auszubildende. Während ich nach der Lehre ging, um Kunst an der Universität zu studieren, blieb er im Unternehmen und arbeitete sich bis in die Geschäftsleitung empor. Wir kauften uns ein Haus und genossen das bessere Leben. Bald darauf heirateten wir und zogen in ein noch größeres Haus. Zwar wusste ich nicht, wozu das nötig war, immerhin waren hundertfünfzig Quadratmeter mehr als genug, aber Daniel war der Meinung, ein „Schloss" würde was hermachen und Geschäftsfreunde wären imponiert. Da er seine Firma repräsentiert, braucht er eben die zweihundertfünfzig Quadratmeter. Dass wir unseren Palast nur zu zweit bewohnen, zählt nicht. Den kann ja eine Putzfrau in Schuss halten und den Garten ein Gärtner.
Logisch, dass ich darauf nicht von allein gekommen bin. Bin halt dumm wie Bohnenstroh. Keine

Ahnung, wie oft mir Daniel das Gefühl gibt, ein gehirnloser Torfkopf zu sein – oft genug, dass ich es selbst glaube.

Ich stehe vorm Spiegel und pudere meine Nase. Dabei starre ich in mein Gesicht und frage mich, ob ich noch attraktiv bin. Seit zwanzig Jahren sind Daniel und ich ein Paar. Ein Kompliment habe ich nie bekommen. Gerne jedoch werde ich mit wachsender Begeisterung von ihm kritisiert. Ich kann es ihm eigentlich nie recht machen, es sei denn, ich schlafe. Da bin ich leise wie eine Feder im Wind und widerspreche nicht. Wehe ich vertrete mal eine andere Meinung als er, dann haben wir sofort wieder eine Diskussion, die sich bis in den späten Abend ausdehnen kann. Grrr, ich hasse dieses Gerede um Nichts! Dabei gibt es so viel Schönes, das man gemeinsam genießen könnte. Aber nein, mein lieber Daniel versteift sich auf unproduktive Wortwechsel, die einem unnötig Energie rauben. Die letzten Jahre frage ich mich immer öfter, was mich eigentlich bei ihm hält. Sein Bankkonto kann es nicht sein. Ich interessiere mich nicht für Geld, es ist mir nicht wichtig. Als wir uns kennenlernten, war er genauso mittellos wie ich. Wir haben unser schlichtes, freies Dasein genossen, sind gern in die Pizzeria nebenan essen gegangen, statt im Sternerestaurant oder haben uns am Kinotag den neuesten Film angesehen. Das Popcorn und die

Getränke schleusten wir heimlich mit ein, um die teuren Preise zu boykottieren. Unsere Klamotten haben wir nach Geschmack ausgesucht und nicht nach dem Label. Wie sehr vermisse ich die alte Zeit, in der wir noch „einfach" waren, ein Paar aus der Mittelschicht, vollkommen durchschnittlich. Jetzt werden die Freunde nach dem Portemonnaie ausgesucht und nicht nach Sympathie. Denn mit weniger gut betuchten Menschen kann Daniel nichts mehr anfangen. Die jammern ja ständig darüber, wie teuer alles sei. Doch für Hartmann, Daniel Hartmann, spielt Geld keine Rolle. Er ist der Obermufti der High Society, gehört zur Crème da la Crème, und das will er auch zeigen. Wo käme man denn da hin, wenn man sich für seinen Reichtum entschuldigen müsste?

Ich seufze und lasse die Puderdose in meine Tasche fallen. Herrje, ich will nicht zurück zum Tisch. Ich könnte einfach umfallen und mich vom Personal zum Taxi tragen lassen. Für einen schwachen Kreislauf kann ich ja nichts. Vielleicht sollte ich noch meinen Lippenstift nachziehen, um die Zeit zu überbrücken. Obgleich ich das gerade gemacht habe. Dabei verabscheue ich es, mir Farbe ins Gesicht zu pinseln. Die gehört auf eine Leinwand und nicht auf die Haut. Aber was soll ich sagen, Daniel legt großen Wert auf eine perfekt gestylte Frau von Stand. Dabei bin ich bloß die unvollkommene Frau von nebenan und möchte das auch gern wieder sein. Hätte ich damals gewusst, was mich mit Herrn Hartmann erwartet, wäre mir niemals in den Sinn gekommen, Frau Hartmann zu werden.

„Leonie?", ruft Daniel von draußen und klopft gegen die Tür der Damentoilette. Ich antworte nicht und überlege, so zu tun, als wäre ich längst weg. Plötzlich öffnet er die Pforte und entdeckt mich bei den Waschbecken. War ja klar, dass er die Unverfrorenheit besitzt, hier einzudringen. „Willst du nicht mal langsam zum Tisch zurückkehren? Wir warten alle auf dich. Das Dessert ist schon serviert worden."

„Ja, ich wollte gerade aufbrechen."

„Hast du mal auf die Uhr gesehen? Du bist bereits eine Viertelstunde weg. Was glaubst du wohl, was das für einen Eindruck macht?"

„Schon mal darüber nachgedacht, was dein Auftritt vorhin für einen Eindruck hinterlassen wird?", kontere ich und würde ihn am liebsten anspringen und ihm in seine überhebliche Visage trommeln.

„Irgendwie musste ich dich doch davor bewahren, noch mehr Unfug von dir zu geben", hält er dagegen. „Jetzt komm endlich, die Hühnerbeine warten." Er grinst bei seiner eigenen Bemerkung, die er enorm witzig findet.

„Die Hühnerbeine können warten, die Hartmänner müssen sich erst streiten!", lasse ich verlauten und bewege mich keinen Zentimeter von der Stelle.

„Hast du vor, mich zu blamieren vor meinen Geschäftskunden?", fragt er aggressiv.

„Das schaffst du auch allein."

„Meine Güte, du bist immer so stur. Hier geht es um Millionen und Madame fühlt sich auf den Schlips getreten."

„Ich fühle mich vor allem nicht ernst genommen."

„Reden wir jetzt über deine verletzten Gefühle?", fragt er und lächelt boshaft. „Also lässt du die Mimose raushängen, ausgerechnet an so einem Tag!" Sein schroffes Lächeln verschwindet. „Prima. Das ist ja wirklich super! Mach nur weiter so und du wirst alles ruinieren!"

Iiiich? Fragend drehe ich mich um. Außer meiner Wenigkeit und Herrn Hartmann ist niemand da. Also wende ich mich ihm wieder zu und zeige mit dem Finger auf mich.

„Meinst du etwa mich?"

„Hallo?", gibt er erhitzt von sich. „Wen denn sonst? Ständig spielst du die Beleidigte, anstatt dir mal klarzumachen, um was es geht!"

„Hier geht es einzig und allein um deine Großspurigkeit, mit der du die Menschen um dich herum niederrennst. Du bemerkst nicht mal, wenn du andere kränkst."

„Ich habe niemanden gekränkt und du bist ja dau-
ernd eingeschnappt."

„Ach so."

„Bewegst du deinen Hintern bitte zurück an den
Tisch?"

Unwillig gehe ich an ihm vorbei und trete in den
Flur. Ich sehe die Hühnerbeine von Weitem, wie
sie sich zuprosten und sich einen Kuss zuwerfen.
Könnte Daniel doch nur eine Spur von der Warm-
herzigkeit besitzen, mit der sich dieses Ehepaar
liebt.

2

Am nächsten Morgen bin ich froh, als Daniel zur Arbeit fährt. Endlich allein. Keine Vorwürfe, kein Gezeter. Nur Ruhe und Frieden. Ich genieße die Zeit ohne ihn. Das sollte mir zu denken geben. Andere vermissen ihren Partner, freuen sich darauf, ihn nach Feierabend zu sehen. Ich dagegen bin dankbar für jede freie Minute. Diese Stille im Haus, das angenehme Rauschen der Heizung, das so meditativ auf mich wirkt. Ich finde das Leben toll – solange Daniel nicht in meiner Nähe ist.

Nach dem Frühstück gehe ich in mein Atelier, das unterm Dach des Hauses liegt. Von dort aus habe ich einen prächtigen Blick auf die Gärten der Nachbarn. Wie sehr ich es liebe, hier oben zu sein und den Pinsel über die Leinwand gleiten zu lassen. Jeder Pinselstrich ist für mich höchste Sinneslust. Das Malen macht mich glücklich, gibt mir die nötige Kraft, die ich brauche, um mich gegen Daniel zu behaupten. Ich bin es leid, mich zu streiten, jedes unnötige Wort möchte ich uns ersparen. Deshalb bin ich im Laufe der Jahre zu einer

Memme mutiert, denn Widerspruch ist zwecklos. Ist man mit einer Kampfmaschine verheiratet, hisst man eines Tages freiwillig die weiße Fahne, um schließlich Ruhe zu haben. Trotzdem genehmige ich mir hin und wieder eine kleine Revolte. Vor allem, wenn es um das Thema „Verreisen" geht. Manchmal erhebe ich Einspruch und bitte um einen Urlaub in den eigenen vier Wänden.

„Ha!", ruft Daniel dann aus. „Das ist doch kein Urlaub. Ich muss fliegen. Möglichst weit weg. Nur so kann ich mich richtig erholen."

„Wie wäre es mit zwei Reisen im Jahr statt fünf?"

„Kommt nicht infrage. So kann ich nicht richtig abschalten."

„Und wenn wir mal in Deutschland urlauben?"

„Willst du mich verkohlen? Ich muss was von der Welt sehen!"

Ja, und jedem erzählen, wo er überall schon war. Denn Prahlen ist Daniels Hobby: *Hey, ich war in Las Vegas, Mexico, China, Japan, England … Ich bin ein Held, denn ich kenne die Welt und kann überall mitreden. Ich bin Daniel, der Columbus des 21. Jahrhunderts.*

Wahrscheinlich ist dieses übertriebene Reiseverlangen der Grund, warum ich nicht mehr so gern in ferne Länder aufbreche. Eigentlich dachte ich mal, mir würde das gefallen. Aber vier- bis fünfmal im Jahr ins Ausland ist einfach zu viel. Entspannung finden wir im Urlaub nie, denn Daniel will möglichst viel sehen, rennt von einer Sehenswürdigkeit zur nächsten. Nur faul am Strand zu liegen, ist nichts für ihn. Da könnte er ja was verpassen. Eigentlich läuft unser gesamtes Leben auf der Überholspur ab, sodass ich mich oft ausgelaugt und verbraucht fühle. Ich sollte mal ein paar Jahrzehnte Pause beantragen, um mich vom Ehestress zu erholen. Bloß wo sollte ich meinen Antrag einreichen? Bis auf Daniel habe ich keinen Chef, weil ich zu Hause arbeite. Meine Malerei wirft nicht viel ab, denn mein großer Durchbruch lässt auf sich warten. Natürlich nimmt mein Mann meine Arbeit nicht ernst, so wie er eigentlich nie etwas ernst nimmt, was ich tue oder sage.

Warum bin ich noch hier?

Diese Frage stelle ich mir immer öfter. Hoffe ich, ihn zu ändern, die alte Zeit eines Tages zurückzuholen? Wäre es so, bin ich eine Traumtänzerin, denn Vergangenes ist vergangen. Menschen lassen sich nicht umformen, und schon gar nicht Daniel. Ich kann ihm keinen Fahrplan in die Hand drücken und sagen: „So, von nun an lenken wir unser Boot in meine Richtung, leben so, wie ich es für uns vorgesehen hab."

So funktioniert das nicht! Denn Daniel lässt sich nichts sagen. Er macht sein Ding. Der Partner muss ihm folgen und nicht umgekehrt!

Das Telefon klingelt. Meine Agentin ruft an. Elli. Na ja, Agentin ist vielleicht ein bisschen hochgestochen. Sie ist meine Freundin und kümmert sich um die Vermarktung meiner Bilder. Bisher war sie damit nicht besonders erfolgreich. Gelegentlich organisiert sie eine Vernissage in einer Kaschemme, aber das führte bisher lediglich zu geringfügigen Verkäufen. Mein Bekanntheitsgrad ist gleich null. Solange ich es nicht schaffe, meine Kunstwerke auf exklusiven Kunst-Events zu präsentieren, sitze ich weiterhin in der zweiten und dritten Reihe, da, wo mich niemand sieht.

„Hey, Leonie", begrüßt sie mich und scheint gut gelaunt zu sein. „Ich habe einen Raum für eine Ausstellung gefunden. Ein ehemaliger Dance-Club im Industriegebiet."

„Oh", sage ich und teile ihre übertriebene Begeisterung nicht. Ein Club im Industriegebiet, eine Gegend, die vollkommen ausgestorben ist, wo sich nicht mal ein Eichhörnchen hin verirrt. Aber ich möchte sie nicht demotivieren und lasse sie meine Dankbarkeit spüren. „Das ist ja toll. Klasse."

„Wenn du willst, können wir uns die Räumlichkeiten nachher mal ansehen. Der Preis, den der Vermieter verlangt, ist human."

„Ach ja?", frage ich und kann mir nicht vorstellen, dass sich die Kosten mit dem Verkauf der Bilder amortisieren werden. Bis jetzt war es fast immer ein Zuschussgeschäft.

„Ja, er verlangt nur 2.500 Euro. Ist das nicht supi?" Ich pruste und schnappe kurz darauf nach Luft.

„Wirklich, supi", antworte ich und überlege, wie ich Daniel überreden kann, mir den Betrag ohne Zänkerei auszuzahlen. Er glaubt nicht, dass meine Bilder gut genug sind, um jemals Anklang in der Kunstwelt zu finden. Er traut mir nicht zu, eine Mallegende zu werden. Ich selbst weiß natürlich genau, dass ich es eines Tages schaffe! Würde ich das nicht glauben, könnte ich kapitulieren. Doch fürs Aufgeben bin ich nicht geschaffen. Ich bin als Kämpferin geboren worden. Dumm nur, dass ich mit einem Kampfhahn verheiratet bin, der mich um Längen schlägt. Ständig meint er, alles besser zu wissen als ich, deshalb pflügt er jegliche meiner Ideen nieder. Er mischt sich in Dinge ein, von denen er nichts versteht, argumentiert mich solange an die Wand, bis ich nachgebe und mich seinen Ansichten füge. Vermutlich mangelt es mir deshalb an Erfolg. Weil ich mich nicht genügend durchsetze, um meinen eigenen Weg zu gehen.

„Und? Treffen wir uns nachher?", will Elli wissen und bedrängt mich eine Spur zu heftig. Eigentlich wollte ich mich den ganzen Tag mit Malen beschäftigen und mich nicht für eine unproduktive Besichtigung in einer Fabrikhalle verabreden. Da ich Elli aber niemals etwas abschlagen kann, stimme ich zu. „Fein", jubelt sie, „dann hole ich dich um dreizehn Uhr ab."

Als es an der Tür schellt, schrecke ich auf und schaue auf die Uhr. Verflucht, ich habe die Zeit total aus den Augen verloren. Sobald ich male, tauche ich in meine Bilder ein und vergesse die Welt um mich herum. Ich lege den Pinsel beiseite und renne vom Dachgeschoss ins Erdgeschoss, um Elli in meiner weißen mit Farbtropfen besprenkelten Latzhose zu öffnen.

„Elli!", rufe ich aus, als ich ihr die Tür öffne. „Ist es schon so weit?"

„Mannomann, Leonie, der Typ erwartet uns um halb zwei. Wie sollen wir das schaffen, wenn du noch nicht fertig bist?"

„Ich bin fertig. Wir können direkt los."

„So?"

„Ja, wo ist das Problem?"

„Na, dein Aufzug!"

„Ach was, das ist schon in Ordnung. Ich will ja keinen Schönheitswettbewerb gewinnen, sondern bloß einen Raum anmieten."

„Wie du meinst. Aber wir fahren mit deinem Auto. Hab keine Lust auf Farbflecke im Polster."

„Klar, machen wir." Ich greife nach dem Wagenschlüssel und meinen Papieren. „Kann losgehen."

3

Pünktlich um halb zwei erreichen wir die still-gelegte Fabrik. Ein junger Mann im Dreiteiler steigt aus seinem offenen Sportwagen und schlendert langsam auf uns zu, während ich mein Auto peinlich genau auf einer eingezeichneten Parkfläche abstelle, was natürlich nicht nötig gewesen wäre, da sonst kein einziges Fahrzeug hier steht.

„Schau mal, Leonie, was da für ein Sahneschnittchen auf uns zukommt."

„Ich sehe nur einen Lackaffen im Designerfummel."

Elli verdreht die Augen über meine Bemerkung und steigt aus, um ihrem Tortenstück entgegenzulaufen. Ich lasse mir Zeit, denn ich hab's nicht eilig. Sobald ich einen Kerl im Anzug sehe, krieg ich das Würgen. Vermutlich liegt's an Daniel, der tagtäglich in perfekter Montur das Haus verlässt und ich diesen Anblick nicht mehr ertragen kann. Obwohl der Anblick nichts dafür kann, lediglich das aufgeblasene Gehabe meines Ehegatten. So-mit sehe ich in jedem Anzugträger einen Snob. Schlimm genug mit einem verheiratet zu sein. Da brauch ich nicht auch noch einem blasierten Hammel auf dem Industriegelände zu begegnen.

Langsam bewege ich mich aus meinem roten Mazda, der in etwa so alt ist wie ich. Ich liebe meine Knutschkugel, weil sie mich niemals im Stich lässt. Natürlich sieht sie nach nichts aus, wirkt wie ein alter Marienkäfer aufgrund ihrer vielen Rostflecke, die ich liebevoll pflege und ausbessere. Aber ich bin Menschen und Gegenständen ein Leben lang treu. Daher tausche ich weder Daniel noch mein Auto aus, auch wenn die Zeit reif wäre. Elli winkt mir von Weitem zu und fordert mich auf, mich zu ihrem Kuchenstück dazuzugesellen. Ich stecke meine Hände in die Taschen der Latzhose und schlürfe angeödet zu ihr und diesem Aufschneider. Ogottogott, seine Parfümwolke erreicht mich schon aus einhundert Meter Entfernung. Ich rümpfe die Nase und mein Unwille, ihm näherzukommen, wird immer größer. Kann Elli das nicht allein aushandeln? Ich hab eine Allergie gegen Sahneschnittchen. Vor allem wenn sie nach Parfümerie stink … äh, duften. Plötzlich verführt der Geruch meine Nase und setzt sich sanft auf meine Flimmerhärchen. Mein Kopf beugt sich von allein vor und scheint sich flinker als der Rest meines Körpers zu bewegen. Nun kann ich nicht schnell genug bei der Süßspeise ankommen, weil sie meinen Geruchssinn mehr umschmeichelt, als mir lieb ist. Ich bin hypnotisiert.

„Frau Hartmann?", spricht mich der Leckerbissen mit seiner Baritonstimme an und ich warte darauf, dass das Orchester mit einstimmt.

„Äh ja, Herr …", flöte ich meinen unvollständigen Satz wie eine Nachtigall. Ich wusste gar nicht, dass meine Stimmbänder solche Töne von sich geben können. Als wäre ich geradewegs aus dem Feenreich entsprungen.

„Rosenbaum", stellt sich die Parfümwolke vor und reicht mir die Hand. „Leon Rosenbaum."

„Leon?", schießt es aus Elli heraus. „Wenn das kein gutes Omen ist. Meine Freundin heißt Leonie."

Plaudertasche!

„Ach, wirklich?", fragt Leon Sahneschnitte. „Was für ein charmanter Zufall."

Ich werde rot. Gott, ich will nach Hause! Raus aus dieser haarsträubenden Situation.

„Ja, in der Tat", sage ich ruppig. „Können wir jetzt zum Geschäftlichen kommen?" …

„Kein Sex mit einem Millionär"
von
Sabine Richling
Erschienen bei BoD als Taschenbuch und
E-Book

Das Leben könnte so schön sein. Wäre Leonie nur nicht mit dem falschen Mann verheiratet. Seit zwanzig Jahren klebt sie an ihrem Angetrauten, der sich zu einem Millionär und überheblichen Patriarchen gemausert hat. Leonie ist Geld nicht wichtig, darum will sie ihr Luxusdasein an den Nagel hängen und endlich wieder „normal" leben – ohne Mann. Doch dann lernt sie Leon, den vermögenden Immobilien-händler, kennen und es knistert gewaltig. Sie wehrt sich ge-gen ihre Gefühle, doch Leon ist ein exzellenter Verführer …

„Verlieben ist Chefsache"
von
Sabine Richling
Erschienen bei BoD als Taschenbuch und
E-Book

**Neuauflage des witzigen Liebesromans „Gefühls-
chaos inklusive"**

Claudia ist wieder Single. Jetzt muss ihr nur noch klar
werden, dass dies ihr Glück ist. Sie will eine angemessene
Zeit um ihre Beziehung trauern. Doch beim ersten Zusam-
menstoß mit dem smarten Oliver wird sie ihren Prinzipien
untreu: Denn dieser sexy Typ ist ein Leckerbissen. Als sie
glaubt, ihr neues Glück gefunden zu haben, melden sich erste
Zweifel. Plötzlich kommt ihr Chef
Christian ins Spiel – attraktiv und faszinierend. Er versteht
es, sie zu umwerben und in Versuchung zu führen …

Amüsante und heitere Liebeskomödie

„Im Jenseits schmeckt die Liebe süßer"
von
Sabine Richling
Erschienen bei BoD als Taschenbuch und
E-Book

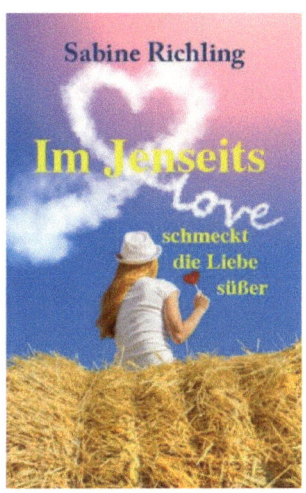

Die siebzehnjährige Lina ist in der Lage, mit Verstorbenen zu reden. Welch verrückte Gabe, die Segen und Fluch zugleich ist!

Dabei will sie nur eines: ein normales Leben führen und den attraktiven Florian näher kennenlernen. Und tatsächlich spricht er sie eines Tages in der Schule an. Er weiß von ihrem Talent und bittet sie um Hilfe. Lina möchte ablehnen, denn so hat sie sich die erste Verabredung mit ihrem Schwarm nicht vorgestellt. Aber sein Charme ist verboten sexy und auch er besitzt eine geheime Begabung.

Als Lina ein rätselhaftes Zeichen aus dem Jenseits erhält, ist sie zutiefst verunsichert. Sie befürchtet, sterben zu müssen. Oder versteht sie alles ganz falsch?

Die spannende Liebesgeschichte voller emotionaler Momente.

Witzig, romantisch und übersinnlich

AUTHOR´S BIO

Sabine Richling was born in 1968 in Berlin. She attended high school and, after completing studies in business administration, she worked for many years in a wholesale establishment. After she had moved to Hamburg, she began her new work for a publishing house. Inspired by the publishing atmosphere, she wrote the first drafts of some short stories. Today she writes primarily romantic comedies and entertaining short stories.